Praise for T

MW01076694

"Weird and heartfelt and hard to pull your eyes away from."
—Stephen Graham Jones, author of *The Buffalo Hunter Hunter*

"With *The Unkillable Frank Lightning*, Rountree solidifies himself as not only one of the best writers working today, but makes the case for being the best Western writer of our present century."
—C. S. Humble, author of *That Light Sublime* trilogy

"This Western reimagining of Shelley's classic sticks true to the heart of the story, while giving us something entirely new and breathlessly exciting."
—Chris Panatier, author of *The Redemption of Morgan Bright*

"Once you start reading *The Unkillable Frank Lightning*, you just won't be able to stop. Catherine Coldbridge and her companions and her Old West are endlessly fascinating."
—Tim Powers, author of *Declare* and *The Stress of Her Regard*

"*The Unkillable Frank Lightning*, much like *The Legend of Charlie Fish*, becomes a kind of paean to the outcast, to the monstrous, and to a land where, once upon a time, there was room enough for them find both love and acceptance."
—*Fan Fi Addict*

"In *The Unkillable Frank Lightning*, Josh Rountree mixes Charles Portis's *True Grit* and Larry McMurtry's *Lonesome Dove* with elements of James Whale's *The Bride of Frankenstein* for a relentless train-ride of a novel."
—Derek Austin Johnson, author of *The Faith*

"Western horror at its finest."
—Bonnie Jo Stufflebeam, author of *Grim Root*

"This is the F-Monster we've always wanted, in a yarn we never knew we needed—until now. Welcome to Josh Rountree's TEX-sylvania!"
—David J. Schow, screenwriter of *The Crow*

"What begins as *The Searchers* meets *Frankenstein* ends as *Unforgiven* meets *The Magicians*."
—C. Robert Cargill, co-screenwriter of *The Black Phone*

"Roundtree continues to hitch his wagon to his unique and fun storytelling genre—the neo-Gothic Western monster mash. His work, as always, is full of heart."
—David Sandner, editor of *The Afterlife of Frankenstein*

"Stands with the best of Charles Portis, Joe R. Lansdale, and Larry McMurtry. Buckle up for a wild ride."
—William Jensen, author of *Cities of Men*

"[*The Unkillable Frank Lightning*], like every damn word I have read from Josh Rountree, is perfection."
—John Boden, author of *The Etiquette of Booby Traps*

"*The Legend of Charlie Fish* was a 'must-read' for us here at *Macabre Daily* and an all-time favorite, and [Rountree's] new novel, *The Unkillable Frank Lightning*, is just as phenomenal."
—*Macabre Daily*

THE UNKILLABLE FRANK LIGHTNING
JOSH ROUNTREE

The Unkillable Frank Lightning
© 2025 by Josh Rountree

Cover and interior design by Elizabeth Story
Author photo by Leah Muse

Tachyon Publications LLC
1459 18th Street #139
San Francisco, CA 94107
415.285.5615
www.tachyonpublications.com
tachyon@tachyonpublications.com

Series editor: Jacob Weisman
Editor: Richard Klaw

Print ISBN: 978-1-61696-436-8
Digital ISBN: 978-1-61696-437-5

Printed in the United States by Versa Press, Inc.

First Edition: 2025
9 8 7 6 5 4 3 2 1

THE
UNKILLABLE
FRANK LIGHTNING

JOSH ROUNTREE

TACHYON • SAN FRANCISCO

Also by the Author

Novel

The Legend of Charlie Fish (2023)

Collections

Can't Buy Me Faded Love (2008)
Fantastic Americana (2021)
Death Aesthetic (2024)

For my parents, my grandparents,
and all my other teachers.

"This isn't science. It's more like black magic."
—Dr. Frankenstein, *Bride of Frankenstein*

"Yesterday's gone on down the river and you can't get it back."
—Larry McMurtry, *Lonesome Dove*

"This is the West, sir. When the legend becomes fact, print the legend."
—Maxwell Scott, *The Man Who Shot Liberty Valance*

Texas on a Fast Train

From the Arkansas Woods to Dallas, Texas
Spring 1905

I NEVER IMAGINED myself the sort of woman to throw in with a pair of killers, but Frank's death unmoored me from the stable life I'd known, and I'd spent the ensuing years shedding every trace of civility and decorum that my society parents had bred into me. The Sioux arrows that killed Frank stole my life as well, and yet I couldn't allow simple human grief to excuse my actions in the wake of his death, or to forgive the life I'd lived since then. Everyone loses people they love. Most of them, however, consign those souls to eternity. They mourn and move on. They don't lose themselves in their own carefully crafted afterlives. And they certainly don't summon their husbands back from the dead.

I have made mistakes that can't be forgiven.

We rode a train to Texas, a place I'd never been, and one I had no desire to visit. In my imagination, Texas was a hard, unforgiving vista of rock and fallow earth. A land that celebrated horse thieves and murderers and anyone else seeking asylum from the civilized world. The prospect of Texas thrilled my wicked companions, and that was enough to turn me off the place. I considered Texas might be my own personal Hell, and knew it was better than I deserved.

"Are you comfortable, Dr. Coldbridge?"

Aubrey Dawson sat beside me. The train shuddered and rocked, carved a straight line through a forest of towering Arkansas pines and clawing cedars that seemed to suck all the oxygen from the train car. The air was moist and hot, and smelled like decay. Sunlight was scarce, and shadows blossomed. I longed for the trees to vanish and the plains to open wide before us so I might breathe again. Aubrey suffered no such claustrophobia. He sat by the window, eternally smiling, like he shared some secret with the forest that the rest of us would never understand. Despite the heat, he kept his blue jacket buttoned tight over his waistcoat and his gray felt hat tipped back at the perfect rakish angle. He was dangerously handsome with his beard clipped neat and his eyes like cold blue gemstones. He was mannered, and at times pleasant, but despite his best efforts, the low man inside him peered out from time to time, revealing the unsavory aspects of his nature.

"Yes, I'm quite fine, Aubrey," I said.

"Offer you a drink?" Aubrey withdrew a tin flask from his pocket and waved it in my direction. I had become quite familiar with that flask in our travels and was grateful for the offer. Given free rein, I'd drink the whole thing in a series of furious swallows, but like Aubrey, there were aspects of myself that I preferred to keep hidden when possible.

"Just a sip, I guess."

Aubrey handed me the flask, and I took a bit more than a sip.

"I like a woman who'll have a nip of whiskey now and again." He retrieved his flask from my reluctant hand, took a drink, and returned it to his pocket.

"And I like men who don't comment on my base proclivities. I suppose I'm destined for disappointment."

"Nothing wrong with enjoying yourself," he said.

"I never said I liked it. I was thirsty."

"We're all of us thirsty, all the time it seems."

"I like you better when you keep quiet," I said.

That drew laughter from the seat across the aisle. Aubrey's brother, Seth, lounged with his hat down over his eyes, but he'd obviously been following our conversation. The Dawson brothers claimed to be twins, but there appeared little relation between them. Aubrey enjoyed his finery, but Seth's black coat was disheveled and stashed in the seat beside him, his shirt untucked except where it would interfere with his holster. Aubrey chose a particular cologne that he mail ordered from Boston, and he existed in a fog of sage and sandalwood, while Seth smelled only of his unwashed body, and often of whiskey. Having spent the last week in their company, I was convinced the creator had doled out all the manners and good looks in their family to Aubrey, and had left Seth begging for the scraps. Despite that, Seth seemed always in good humor, and I'd yet to experience his shadow side, though I suspected that was at least one quality he shared with his brother.

"Aubrey is usually the quiet sort," said Seth. "You must bring out the talker in him. He's often too reserved for his own good."

"I'll admit, it's a character flaw I can't overcome."

"I suppose it's not the talking I mind," I said, "it's what you have to say."

Seth laughed all the harder, and Aubrey didn't let his smile slip for a second.

Under other circumstances, I might not have felt comfortable being so bold in their company. Might, in fact, have feared for my life. But I paid them five hundred dollars each before our departure, and I'd promised to double that amount upon our return to St. Louis. A hedge against them deciding to take my money and leave unfinished the job for which I'd hired them. So, if for no other reason than simple greed, I believed they'd endure a measure of my unpleasant personality, my ribbing, and my naked disdain. I was without love or happiness, and rarely chased those things anymore. But I had plenty of money, and that was enough to keep a person moving forward through life, if they were skilled enough at self-deception to pretend all those other things didn't matter.

Aubrey went back to looking out the window, kept his palm rested on his pistol, as he always did. I reminded myself these were not my friends. They were a hard pair. Alleged killers. And they'd have no problem burying me too if circumstances demanded.

Thankfully I was years past caring what became of me.

"I'd like another drink," I said.

"I'm sure you would," said Aubrey.

"Can I have another, is what I'm asking."

"Well, as long as you're asking nice."

This time I took the flask and drained it. I did my best to wait a while between sips, to pretend there was no urgency in my gut that demanded to be sated. I disguised myself as a proper lady with my bustle in place and my corset drawn tight as a clenched fist around my midsection. My forest green hat matched my dress. I kept it fastened to my head with a fat ribbon, and my graying chestnut hair was knotted up beneath it. But I could only play at being the person I used to be so much. I ignored Aubrey's satisfied look when I handed him the empty flask. I closed my eyes and enjoyed the swimmy feeling in my head as the liquor sought out my bloodstream. Despite my efforts, Aubrey and Seth had figured out exactly the person I was, and I wasn't sure why I continued to put on airs.

I lazed in the seat for a long time. Maybe I slept. The motion of the train became a steady comfort, and as rain began to patter against the top of the car, I experienced dreams or visions. It was hard to tell which anymore. Summoning my husband's soul back into his broken body had required me to reach out my mind to a darker corner of reality, and while doing so, I'd disturbed something that had haunted me through the intervening years. White as the face of the moon and just as featureless. Slender as a willow tree with limbs that stretched and flowed like milky blood though the veins of the world. The creature lived in my dreams and in the periphery of my waking hours, visible in the silvery reflection of old mirrors and coiling through the bustle of crowded streets. Never revealing itself in full, but always haunting me.

No matter how much whiskey, no matter how powerful the dose of laudanum, it remained a near-constant companion, and the only explanation I could surmise was that I'd awoken some guardian of the afterlife. And it would not sleep again until I'd made some sort of amends. It had taken a long time to work up to what needed to be done, but now that I had, I would not allow myself to be deterred.

"We have arrived, Dr. Coldbridge."

I hadn't realized the train had come to a stop. Hadn't realized that we'd traded pine trees for rolling plains and sprawling oaks somewhere along the way. My mouth was dry, and my head hurt, and I was uncertain exactly how many hours had passed since I closed my eyes.

"Okay, Aubrey," I said. "Rouse your brother, and I'll make arrangements."

A porter unloaded our belongings, and we followed him through the busy streets. I don't know what I was expecting from Dallas, possibly a few hastily assembled clapboard buildings near the train station, but it was a proper city. Not so vital as its eastern cousins, but aspiring to more with its tall stone buildings, grand mansions, and a cupola clock tower lording over it all from many stories above us. Rain had turned the streets to mud, but wagons slopped through the mess and a streetcar rattled past, packed to bursting with people about their afternoon business. An automobile came around the corner, moving at a crawl, the driver with both hands fixed on the steering wheel while a bald man in the passenger seat talked excitedly into his ear. White hot sunshine gilded the proceedings, and the humid air already had me sweating. My clothes clung to me like a skin I desperately needed to shed. My headache was like a giant fist, closing tight around my skull. I wanted nothing more than to escape the sudden chaos of Dallas.

The porter led us to what he called the *finest hotel in town*, a huge domed edifice filled with lush carpets and dusty tapestries that absorbed all sound and made the place feel lifeless as a tomb. A framed poster commemorated President Roosevelt having stayed in that very hotel on his recent travels through Texas. Sunlight struggled through the front windows, joined forces with electric wall sconces to combat the shadows that seemed more at home than any of the footmen and maids hustling about. A severe old woman with an oversized butterfly broach worked the front desk. Her silver hair was pinned back so tightly that it stretched her forehead away from her eyes and gave her the impression of being constantly surprised.

"We require two rooms," I said. "One night."

"You're married?" the old woman asked.

"We're not," I said. "One room for myself, and another for these men."

Aubrey remained close behind me, his constant presence at once overwhelming and a comfort. Seth found an overstuffed blue velvet chair by the window, and sat there, smoking a cigarette, and watching the passersby. As if we had not just spent days on a train, with nothing to do but sit and watch the slow unravelling of the world.

"Where have you traveled from?" The old woman made no move to check us in.

"Missouri," I said. "St. Louis."

"This is a moral establishment," the woman said. "We are very rigid in our rules of propriety. We expect no less from our guests."

"I am glad to hear it."

"The President himself stayed here, you know."

"Is his room available?" asked Aubrey. "I would not mind soiling those same sheets."

The old woman reached behind her, produced a rifle, and placed it on the countertop. "We have no use for criminal types. Or drunks or carousers. We frown on heathenry of any sort."

"We'll take that under advisement," said Aubrey.

"Any room is fine," I said. "Any *two* rooms. I assure you these are hired men, nothing more."

"Hired for what?"

"Bodyguards," I said. "Would you expect a woman to cross the country by herself without someone to look after her safety?"

It was my opinion that women *could* and most often *should* look after their own interests, and by doing so, would find themselves much safer and more comfortable than those who relied solely on men. And I was confident my former occupation as a field doctor attached to the U.S. Cavalry had introduced me to more peril than my *protectors* would ever know. But I was sweaty and worn thin as a sewing needle. My feet hurt and my stomach sloshed about, and I wanted nothing more than to be alone some place cool and dark. So, I played the role she expected of me. A chaste woman afraid of the world. A role I'd grown weary of. But it was enough to dislodge the desk clerk from her position of resistance, and she returned the rifle to its hiding place.

"I suppose not," she said. "If you've no husband to accompany you."

"I haven't."

"Are you a widow, or an old maid?"

"I've never married," I lied.

"Well, I suppose it's too late for that now," she said. "Two rooms, then."

"Excellent."

"I'll have the bell captain guide you."

"Might I also inquire where the *Wild West Revue* is performing? I saw the posters, and I'd like to attend. If you don't think such a diversion would prove overtaxing?"

Aubrey snorted.

The old woman readied two keys and rang for the bell captain. "The show has moved on, thank goodness."

"When?"

"Yesterday. Bunch of ill-mannered, smelly animals and I'm glad our beautiful town is shut of them."

"They've moved on to Fort Worth, then."

"I didn't care to ask."

"Well, thank you for your kind welcome to Dallas."

We followed the bell captain to our rooms, and the old woman had managed to situate us on opposite ends of the long, second-story hallway. As if distance might lessen any earthly temptations. Well, it was too late for that. I'd met Aubrey Dawson two weeks ago and had already invited him into my bed a half dozen times. If the old woman at the front desk knew the things we'd done together, she'd have me tossed in the street. But I was beyond caring what people like her thought of me. What *anyone* thought of me. And I was utterly uninterested in her code of morals. She could keep all that fear of judgement and punishment to herself. I knew more about the afterlife than she ever would. Death wasn't fiery torment or angel choirs. Death wasn't an endless, black forever.

Death wasn't even *final*, no matter how much I might wish it was.

I dispatched Aubrey on an errand, and he returned fifteen minutes later with a pint of whiskey. I cracked the door, let him hand it through to me.

"Seth and I are going to see what this town has to offer," he said. "Care to accompany us?"

"No, you go ahead," I said. "I need to meditate before I drink myself to sleep."

"You're an uncommon woman."

"Is that a compliment or an insult?"

"More of an observation," he said. "You want me to bring you dinner?"

I shook the pint bottle. "This will suffice."

"Shall I call on you later this evening?"

"I don't believe that would be wise."

"I'll knock when I get back, just in case."

I closed the door.

My room was small and crammed tight with overlarge oak furniture. The lace curtains were yellowed and drawn, allowing little of the afternoon light to infiltrate. Floral wallpaper covered the walls, red as arterial blood, and cobwebs gathered in the corners. Lavender sachets were tossed about to cover the encroaching smell of mildew. I wasn't certain how my room ranked among the others at the hotel, but I suspected this was not the suite that had hosted President Roosevelt. No matter. There was space enough for my meditation, and the bed appeared soft. Anything more would be a distracting luxury.

My battered leather doctor's bag contained everything needed to conduct field surgery, as well as odds and ends necessary for more esoteric pursuits. I uncapped the whiskey and drank half the bottle. Unbuckled the bag and inhaled a melody of scents that sang my mind into a more peaceful place. I withdrew every ritual element I needed and arranged them just so. Colored candles and cut stones—onyx and quartz and lapis lazuli. Dried plants and scattered animal bones. With everything in place, I made myself comfortable. Removed each dusty, travel-stained layer of clothing until only my cotton chemise remained. Relished the uncomplicated feeling of my bare feet against the hotel's smooth sanded floorboards. Shadows cooled the room, and when I lit the candles, the darkness began to whirl and dance. I blew out the match, inhaled the sulfur. Arranged myself comfortably on the floor with my legs crossed and applied a perfume of my own manufacture to my wrists and my throat.

I downed the rest of the whiskey.

Closed my eyes and found a steady rhythm to my breathing.

Then I summoned up an image of my husband. Not the soft-spoken man with friendly green eyes and easy laugh that I'd known at Fort Ellis. That version of Frank died in Montana, and I should have left him that way. Instead, I imagined the violent, bloody killer that inhabited the new body I'd built for him. The killer I'd unleashed on the world.

Love and grief had motivated me then.

Now it was simple terror that insisted I undo it.

The killer's image firmed up in my mind, greenish and mapped with scars. The world around him came into soft focus, and I saw a young boy with a pistol on each hip, dogging his heels. Cattle massed around them. Tent posts rose and the sound of hammers rang out. Campfires danced in my vision, and the smell of woodsmoke and gunpower suffused the hotel room. The killer and the boy spoke to one another, but it was nothing more than a buzz and a murmur to my senses. I pressed myself closer, felt the heat of the afternoon on my shoulders, and the endless wind riding in from the plains as it tossed my hair. For a second, the killer seemed to sense me, and his eyes widened, like a ghost had passed in front of him. Then the chaos of their camp spiraled around them, and the colors in my mind began to run like rain down a windowpane.

I struggled to keep the connection, though I don't know why. It had taken me years to build my abilities to the point where I could find Frank. Once I learned he'd joined *Cowboy Dan's Wild West Revue*, it was only a matter of reading the newspaper advertisements to determine where he'd be travelling next. They had moved on from Dallas, which meant they were in Fort Worth, only thirty or so miles away.

Most likely, I'd see him the next day.

But I still couldn't help myself, opening my mind and peering into his world.

Part of it was my simple curiosity, but there was also an addictive quality to visiting what my mentor had called the *astral plane*. Becoming free from the kingdom of earth for a time always proved beautiful and strange, and so very hard to resist. Particularly when one was little enamored of her everyday existence.

With concentration, the killer and the boy came into view again, and I chased after them, uninterested in their mundane pursuits, but content to simply *exist* in this other place for a time. Drifting and light and free from worry. The killer appeared jovial and almost fatherly around the boy, and I reminded myself there existed a trail of dead souls that had gazed upon that face and seen their own violent deaths. No matter his appearance, the killer still held darkness within him.

He owed eternity a death, and payment had come due.

The familiar white specter appeared in my mind like a deadly flower unfolding from graveyard soil. It banished the images of the *Wild West Revue* and the heat of the afternoon. Reached out to me with willowy limbs, like it meant to pull me into the afterlife and hold me forever. I withdrew myself at once from that ethereal place and returned to the hard world. I blew out every candle. Whispered thanks to the four elements and pressed my palms against the floorboards to feel the firmness of the world around me. Placed my forehead against the ground until my breathing stilled, and my heart quit trying to escape my chest.

Nighttime had arrived while I was in that other place, and some hours had passed. My stomach growled, and I wished I'd taken Aubrey up on his offer of food. I packed everything back into my bag and lay on top of the bedcovers without the benefit of candlelight. City noises carried up to my room as the denizens of Dallas caroused beneath the streetlights. When Aubrey knocked on my door, deep in the night, I pretended to be asleep. I was in no mood for his fumbling affections.

Tomorrow we'd head to Fort Worth to kill a man.

And I wasn't sure any of us would be coming back.

Far as the Eye Can See

Fort Ellis, Montana Territory
Autumn 1879

FRANK HUMBLE RODE TO HIS DEATH not two weeks after we joined our hands beneath a stand of ponderosa pines and pledged our lives to one another.

Our union was blessed by a Methodist minister no older than eighteen, a boy named Paul Meek, recently arrived from Chicago to replace the old minister, who'd tumbled off a wagon, snapped his shinbone, and died of the resulting infection. Fort Ellis was a hard place, not kind to anyone, not even those with God on their side. During the service, the boy went on at length about how human lives were like candle flames, easily extinguished. How love was more fragile, still. Myriad dangers lurked in the heathen wilderness, all eager to ruin our happiness. But Frank and I didn't share his fear of the world, and we had no expectations that his pessimism would bear fruit. Preacher Meek could not know what it was to be in love. Could not know the sort of hope love invested in a person.

He feared God, and seemingly everything else.

But he could not know our future.

Low clouds draped the distant mountains. Blue morning fog carried in from the foothills, and the cold autumn wind smelled of juniper and cook smoke. Frank and I grinned at one another, let the preacher's terrors pass over us and vanish. Our ceremony was a stolen moment; we both had responsibilities requiring our attention, but neither of us wanted to wait any longer. Fort Ellis churned behind us as we traded our vows in the tall grass outside the palisades. Horses clomped and soldiers assembled. Voices shouted from the barracks and beeves fresh in from Bozeman lowed in mournful voices. The wind quickened, tossed my skirts, and whipped the stars and stripes on the tall wooden flagpole. Despite the chill, Frank's hands were hot in mine, and I could feel the movement of the blood within him. I understood his excitement, and my heart answered, galloping along at a furious pace. There was nothing I wanted more than to marry this man I'd loved for six months, and the bloodless worries of a virgin preacher would not derail our plans.

The world sang with life.

Death could never harrow us.

Frank wore his blue cavalry uniform, and I wore a long gray dress with tall black boots, the closest thing the Army had to a woman's surgeon's uniform available at Fort Ellis. Women doctors were scarce, particularly this far west, but I knew enough people in high places who were still quite fond of my late parents, and though they hadn't understood my desire to leave the east, they'd advanced my cause with the Army. Little remained for me in Philadelphia. Nothing kept me there apart from a loyalty to my parents, but tuberculosis had stolen them away, and left me eager to go someplace where their memory would pain me less. And the West had seemed a place where I might indulge my esoteric talents without oversight, though standing there with the young preacher droning on, I wondered if the wilderness itself might be the only place to escape the watchful eye of civilization.

I had not come to Montana searching for love. Only for a place and a purpose. I could not remember a time in my life where I felt the affections of a man were necessary to my happiness.

Frank was an entirely unexpected revelation.

When the time came, he placed a ring on my finger. It was an unadorned silver band that shimmered like the surface of a river in the daylight, a gift that would remain bound to me long after Frank was dead, and I'd given up hopes of salvaging a life. It was a talisman to conjure faded memories of lost love and dashed ambitions. For decades, I would twist the band around my finger, hoarding every memory I had of that beautiful young man who should never have ridden west. He was quite tall, broad shouldered and muscled, but his manner was too gentle and his heart too kind to survive such a harsh land. Certainly, he could have discovered better prospects in his home state of New York, but three generations of Humble men had preceded him in the United States Army. His father became a decorated hero at the Battle of Buena Vista, and his grandfather served under General Harrison in the War of 1812. His great-grandfather, at least according to family legend, bloodied the British at Yorktown, and sent them packing. And so, service was expected of Frank Humble as well. He'd not been old enough to fight the rebels in the Civil War, and the fact that there was no war to define his son caused Frank's father no end of consternation.

But protecting the frontier from Indians? Well, his father considered that quite the noble cause, even if Frank's sympathies lay elsewhere. Nothing but this familial obligation would have compelled Frank to join the Army, and to allow that Army to march him to the frayed edges of civilization. Frank approached his enlistment with designs on treating with the Indians rather than killing them. And while he'd undertaken a great deal of that treating during his time in the Dakotas, and now in Montana, it was the killing that had consumed him. The leaders he followed often lacked patience, and treaty after worthless treaty had caused the Sioux and the Arapaho and the Cheyenne to answer attempts at relocation with violence. By the time I met Frank, he'd spent seven years fighting in the mountains, trading carbine fire across grassy plains, and digging graves in the badlands. He'd not lost his desire for peace, but he'd come to understand that the fundamental motives of western expansion could never dovetail with the culture and the environmental needs of the native people. The whole experience had hardened him. Frank could no longer foresee any outcome other than native extinction, and the prospect sickened him.

Frank wanted nothing more than to leave the west, but when our destinies are chosen for us, few have the strength to argue. And while he'd marched west unwillingly, and I'd purposely fled my home in search of a new one, we were both ill-suited for life at Fort Ellis. Capable in our duties for certain, but unhappy with our circumstances.

It was this shared condition, more than anything else, that bound us so tightly together.

These melancholy thoughts only haunted me in later years. I prefer to remember our pine-shrouded wedding as a moment of unchecked optimism, if not understandable naivete.

Our plan was to leave Fort Ellis within the year, when Frank had honored his commitment to the Army. Neither of us had designs on any particular destination. Our only requirement was that we build our life somewhere far from Montana. Chicago or Boston or New Orleans—they were all equally enticing. We had only to choose a direction and let fate guide us to a better place.

But we'd never go any of those places together.

The West would break us both.

Frank and I exchanged our vows, kept our hands clasped as we looked into one another's eyes, unwilling to acknowledge the trauma the frontier had already inflicted on us both. And when Paul Meek finished his preaching, and allowed us to kiss in the cold pine shade, Frank and I laughed, delirious in our union.

That night, we consummated our marriage in the small room I lived in, behind the hospital building. We entangled ourselves in love.

Two weeks later, the frontier tore us asunder.

On the day Frank rode out from Fort Ellis for the last time, he visited me in the hospital. When he arrived, I was arguing with my colleague, the tiresome Dr. Prosper, over the deteriorating condition of one Corporal Leonard Levi, who'd arrived back to the fort a week prior with an arrow protruding from his thigh, and whose entire leg had proceeded to leak blood and blacken despite our careful ministrations. Dr. Prosper believed the leg required immediate amputation. He'd served as a field surgeon in the war, and he eagerly advocated for amputation, whenever possible. Soldiers joked they were unwilling to visit the doctor for headache medicine, for fear he would recommend decapitation. Corporal Levi would, most likely, lose the leg. But unlike Dr. Prosper, I was not ready to concede this outcome. I had medicines and rituals yet untried, and felt my magickal skills might blaze a path to wellness that our collective medical understanding was not entirely ready to follow. But talk of magickal healing in mixed company would likely lead to my dismissal from duty, and so I tried to buy more time with Dr. Prosper, while not revealing the extent of my motives.

"One more day," I said. "I believe the poultice is working."

Dr. Prosper snorted. "Poultice. His leg seethes with decay. He won't survive unless we deploy the bone saw."

"I assure you, this is potent medicine," I said. "I've seen it break infections like this before."

"Potent medicine, taught at that august place of learning, the Woman's Medical College of Pennsylvania?" He said this in such a dismissive fashion, I longed to strike him in the face. Dr. Prosper never smiled, yet his eyes always seemed amused when we discussed my medical schooling. He wore tiny spectacles, and his graying hair was shaggy, spilling over his shirt collar. He drank throughout the day, taking no pains to hide it, claiming the liquor calmed his nerves and ensured a steady hand, in the event that an infected limb required removal.

"The Woman's Medical College of Pennsylvania is a highly respected school."

"I'm sure it is."

"Dr. Prosper, you are not the only one here with extensive medical training."

"Yet I am the only one here who realizes his limitations."

"Perhaps these are limitations we don't share."

"You are married now, aren't you, Dr. Coldbridge? Or is it Dr. Humble now?"

"You know I'm married."

"Then don't you have marital duties to perform?"

"Such as?"

"Keeping a home for your husband? Planning for children. We are quite capable of providing quality medical care to our patients here without your assistance. I'm sure he would prefer you to attend to him in the evenings, instead of sitting by this man's bedside at all hours, endeavoring to heal him with your quaint folk remedies."

"Trying to save his life, you mean."

"Ah, and here he is now," said Dr. Prosper. "Your lord husband. No doubt come to explain how you can be of service in some capacity other than medicine."

Frank stood in the threshold with the door half-open, motioning for me to come to him. He knew better than to enter the room. Dr. Prosper tended to chase away any nonmedical personnel with vituperative vigor. Falling Bird stood behind Frank, peeking also into that forbidden space. There existed only two patients at that time, Corporal Levi, and another soldier, who had begun vomiting in the night, and had yet been unable to stop. It was unlikely that Frank or Falling Bird would stand in the way of either man's healing process, but Dr. Prosper would suffer no others in his sanctuary, and the mere sight of Falling Bird lurking behind Frank was enough to rile the doctor into a mild fit.

"Please wait outside, sir!" he said. "And your Indian can wait there with you."

"I'll be back shortly," I said. "Please refrain from removing this man's leg until I've returned."

"I promise nothing."

Outside, I allowed myself a moment to luxuriate in the fading warmth of a glorious autumn sunshine. Such comfort was fleeting. Soon the winds would grow angry and cold, and the snows would chase away even the memory of sunshine. Fort Ellis continued preparations for the coming winter; men moved about in the yard, undertaking their duties with alacrity. The single-story hospital stood near a long row of sturdy barracks, and across the parade yard from the commissary and the small, whitewashed church where Preacher Meek plied his heavenly wisdom.

Frank hugged me in greeting, like he hadn't seen me in a while, though we'd shared breakfast just that morning. When he spoke, I realized it wasn't a greeting, but a farewell.

"We're mustering for patrol," he said.

"You're leaving? When?"

"Today," he said. "Though I don't expect to be gone more than a few days. Our reasons for going are spurious, in my opinion."

Falling Bird laughed. "You'll make a diplomat yet."

Falling Bird was a Crow man, deep in the throes of middle age, but lively as any youth despite his constant claims of misfortune and maladies. He was a sure rider, a scout and interpreter for the Army, and according to Frank, the savior of more than one ill-considered patrol into hostile territory. The two men were fast friends. Or perhaps Frank looked on Falling Bird as a father figure in some ways. I never knew for sure, but they were joined at the hip when in camp, and they'd ridden enough miles together that their bond was one of blood and mutual sacrifice.

Falling Bird wore the boots and trousers of the military, but above that he wore an elk hide shirt adorned with beads, and an ancient buffalo coat that fell all the way to his ankles. His black hair was streaked with gray, and tied back in a tail with a leather thong. A long knife hung from one hip, and a pistol from the other. Frank had shared stories of the tight situations they'd endured together, but I could scarcely imagine someone as unfailingly courteous as Falling Bird making use of either weapon.

I suppose the same could be said for my dear husband, but there was no escaping the fact that his gentle hands had taken more than one life.

The West changed us. We became different people entirely. No return to our former selves was possible.

I didn't understand that then, but I know it with a certainly now.

"Someone attacked a buckboard," said Frank. "Just the other side of Bozeman. Killed the kid driving it, took the horses. Probably whatever else he was carrying too. More likely than not, the culprit is some unremarkable species of thief and killer. But someone with a higher rank than mine believes with a certainty that Indians are to blame, and this attack presages an incursion by rampaging Sioux. So, we get to spend a few days in the saddle, chasing ghosts and proving they're wrong."

"You make it sound like a chore," said Falling Horse. "It's better than standing around this place for weeks on end. The longer I'm out of the saddle, the more my back pains me. Riding cures everything."

Fort Ellis had been untroubled by the Sioux or any other tribe of late, and it was the general sentiment that hostilities on the northern plains were rapidly approaching an end. Certainly, the notion of Indians raiding around Bozeman wasn't far-fetched, but I'd allowed myself to believe the danger was passing.

Frank had ridden out several times since we'd met, but never since we'd been married. Had I foolishly thought our union would put an end to his dangerous duties?

I wanted more than ever to leave this place with him at my side, and never return.

"When are you leaving?" I asked.

"Within the hour," said Frank.

"Can I trouble you for some of your ointment?" asked Falling Bird. "My back truly is on fire."

"Yes, I'll get you a bottle to take along with you."

"Your kindness is appreciated," he said.

"Well, you can repay me by bringing my husband home alive,"

"We'll be fine," said Frank.

"Unless we aren't," said Falling Bird.

"I know you're joking to tame my fears," I said, "but it's not working."

"We look after one another," said Falling Bird. "We always do. I promise you that much."

"There are twelve of us riding out in search of what is surely a lone bandit," said Frank. "Sioux or Arapaho or a white man trying to blame them, it doesn't matter."

"Unless it's more than one," I said.

"Yeah, unless that."

"Let me get my bag, I'll ride along with you. Never can tell when you may require a doctor's services."

"Can't happen," said Frank. "The captain has already mustered everyone he's taking."

"I can talk to the captain."

"Catherine, I promise this is just a quick trip."

"We are both too pretty to kill," said Falling Bird.

"That's hardly the case," I said.

There was no use arguing. I might talk myself onto the patrol, but I could not live Frank's life for him, could not remain by his side every moment of the day to keep him safe. For the first time since Philadelphia, I considered what a heavy burden love could be, and wondered if it would get any lighter as our time together progressed.

I peeked back into the hospital, to make sure Dr. Prosper hadn't bothered Corporal Levi overmuch, then I walked with Frank and Falling Bird to the parade grounds and watched the men preparing for patrol. When it was time for their departure, I embraced Frank with all my strength as if absorbing the memory of his shape into my being. I didn't really think it would be our last embrace, but I was worried enough by the prospect of his leaving to consider it as such, just in case. When the gates opened and they rode off, none of the men looked back. They followed the captain out into that dangerous world of hard circumstances and uncertain outcomes. A place where my prayers could not reach, and my hopes would never find purchase.

They were well armed; they rode sprightly horses.

They were bound by duty and pride.

And in the end, none of that would make a difference.

Fort Worth Blues

Along the Trinity River to Fort Worth, Texas
Spring 1905

WE TRAVELED TO FORT WORTH on horseback rather than wait for the train. The Trinity River was our guide, and our horses galloped across a vista of windblown grass, deep and lush, beneath an angry gray sky that threatened rain. Lightning lanced through the clouds, not far to the north, and thunder chased us across the prairie like a pack of growling dogs. The Dawson brothers questioned my readiness to ride, suggesting perhaps the thirty miles on horseback would be a hardship I would not care to endure. So, I set the pace. Made them keep up. Disabused them of any notion that my womanhood was limiting. My backside had spent more hours in the saddle than theirs, I wagered. And though I'd just turned fifty-three years old, I was as sure a rider as I'd been in my youth, when I'd raced for my life beneath the endless Montana skies.

In that moment, I felt fearless.

Aubrey was sullen. Red-eyed and weary. Whatever indulgences the brothers had undertaken the night before, it was clear he was paying a physical price for it. Hooves beat against the earth, and Aubrey's horse bounced beneath him. He clung to the pommel with both hands, like he feared being tossed into that sea of grass and lost forever. He'd neglected his beard, and his face was sallow. All morning, he'd been quiet. My refusal to answer his knock the night before was a point of contention, but it was evident he was in no shape for physical activity, and I doubted either of us would have taken much pleasure.

Seth was grinning. Light in the saddle. He'd gone with me to arrange purchase of the horses an hour before his brother had opened his eyes to harsh daylight. Seth's vices had not slowed him, and I'd woken with not even a headache. This left Aubrey feeling vexed by us both, his shoulders alone bearing the weight of all our sins.

About halfway there, we stopped along the riverbank to give the horses a rest, and let them drink.

Seth and I dismounted, moved around, and stretched our legs. Aubrey stayed in the saddle.

"I believe you've overindulged." Seth slapped Aubrey's leg, clearly enjoying his brother's discomfort. "Your face is green as a mallard duck."

"I'm fine," said Aubrey.

"I myself feel quite refreshed today," said Seth.

"No doubt from clean living," said Aubrey.

"Not so clean. Not always."

"Can we proceed?" said Aubrey. "We're killing daylight."

"I thought you'd appreciate the temporary reprieve," I said. "Forgive me, but you don't look comfortable in the saddle. Have you much experience riding?"

Seth cackled, and Aubrey gunned me down with his bleary stare. "I'm experienced enough, Dr. Coldbridge. In all manner of things."

"I'm sure you are."

"You've hired us for a service," he said. "I'd like to be about that business so I can go home. I'm not fond of the wilderness."

"Think of it as a grand adventure," I said. "Surely the whole undertaking isn't that bad?"

"I'll admit to some few enjoyable diversions."

"I'm glad to hear it."

"Doesn't mean I want to linger here," he said.

"Don't blame Aubrey, Doc," said Seth. "It's not his fault he prefers to do his killing in the big city. That's just how he was raised."

Aubrey found his smile again. "Guilty as charged."

Wind rustled through a stand of juniper trees lined along the far side of the river, and the thunder spoke up again. The day was warm, but the wind was cold, a whispered warning of the approaching storm. Being set loose in the wide world on horseback had caused me to feel young again, invested with more life than I'd become accustomed to. In the claustrophobic heart of a city, death might be watching from every open alley, peering through any storefront window. Death might mingle in any crowd and make its slow approach unchecked. Beneath this open sky, there was hope a person might see her fate coming before it arrived, have an opportunity to act. And so, I took pleasure in being there; I allowed myself to relax.

But Seth's casual comment banished my good mood.

Here I was alone with two admitted killers, pistols hanging like guillotines from their belts. All of us laughing at one another's sins.

Maybe hours away from killing a man I used to love.

If death wasn't here already, we'd brought it with us.

But of course, that was foolishness. My fleeting sense of freedom and safety had been nothing but self-deception. Death had arrived in this place long ago. When the horses plunged their hooves into the red clay at the edge of the river, it called to mind blood spilled and bodies torn. Gun smoke and terror and flint-tipped arrows hissing through the air. Charred bodies and wails of grief. This wasn't Montana; this was Texas. But it was still *the West*. And though five years had passed in a new century, the conflicts of the old one remained vivid. I doubted they would ever leave us. Violence lived in the firmament of the country like a seam of silver running through a mine. It was in the land, and it was in the people, and there was nothing we could do to escape it.

I had given up trying long ago.

I closed my eyes, tried to breathe in some peace.

"Are you troubled, Dr. Coldbridge?" Aubrey's tone suggested he sensed the change in my mood, and now he had the upper hand. I could feel the smile in his voice, even with my eyes closed.

"Just enjoying the breeze," I said.

"We'll be enjoying a lightning strike if we don't move along soon," said Seth.

"Just another second." Anxiety churned inside me. My addictions hadn't called to me that morning, but they spoke up loud and insistent in that moment.

"Feel free to stay awhile," said Aubrey. "I'm riding."

He spurred his horse, and trotted away.

Seth mounted up, followed his brother.

There was nothing to do but join them. I trailed close behind as they picked up the pace, headed farther west.

We arrived in Fort Worth by midafternoon, but the thunderstorm beat us there. Curtains of rain marched through the streets as we rode into town, soaking us to the bone. Lightning splintered right over top of us, and the thunder came down like a hammer. We trudged through the miserable, muddy streets until we located a livery to stable our horses, then hurried over to the questionable sanctuary of a place called the Silver Ace. We stood on the covered porch of that establishment to catch our breath and get our bearings. I had with me only my leather medical bag and a few sundries, the rest of my belongings having been left at the hotel in Dallas for my return. I'd expected our trip to Fort Worth to be short, but killing Frank would require finding him first, and any performances he had scheduled that day would certainly be canceled due to weather.

"We appear to be in the right place." Seth pointed at an advertising poster hanging in the window.

It was the same poster I'd seen in Dallas and other locales. COWBOY DAN'S WILD WEST REVUE emblazoned in large letters across the top. Gunfighters amid puffs of blue smoke, Indians with feathered lances, and cowboys with their lassos twirling overhead, all chasing one another in a circle. In the middle of it all rested a brightly colored drawing of Cowboy Dan himself. It was evident he possessed a powerful envy of that great impresario Buffalo Bill Cody, for he styled himself after the man, as if by affecting the same long white hair and stylish beard, people might hold him in similar esteem. In the bottom corner of the poster appeared a stylized drawing of a massive, hulking man with no face, hands upraised at the sky, fingers splayed. Arrows sticking out of his back. Beneath this drawing the sign read: FEATURING THE UNKILLABLE FRANK LIGHTNING. WANTED DEAD OR ALIVE! OR BOTH!

The Unkillable Frank Lightning.

I closed my eyes, took a breath.

That remained to be seen.

Tiny hailstones began to rattle against the metal awning, driving us inside.

The Silver Ace was not unlike the place in St. Louis where'd I'd met the Dawson brothers and set this entire endeavor in motion. A grimy saloon with a low-slung ceiling and watered-down whiskey, dank with shadows and choked with smoke. Electric lights buzzed from wall sconces, faded on and off as the storm raged harder. Cowboys crowded the bar, muddy boots hooked on the brass rail, tossing back whiskey shots and talking over one another in too-loud voices. Others gathered around scattered tables, playing faro or chewing on steak lunches. The air inside was heavy, laced with the sour smell of spilled liquor and dirty people. I was keenly aware that we'd ridden into the part of town everyone called Hell's Half Acre, and I suspected the Dawson brothers had chosen this neighborhood for its dark reputation. No doubt the place had been a whore house in Fort Worth's earlier, wilder days. Might even still have been one. But it was dry, and there were rooms along the upstairs landing for let, so I decided it would suffice for our short stay.

Seth located a mostly clean table, and we ordered a few of those steaks. A flickering oil lantern sat in the middle of the table, working overtime to make up for the shortcomings of the wall sconces. We were soaked and uncomfortable, sore from the ride and impatient for the completion of our task. I'd found that when I let my momentum slip, when I considered the intricacies of what I intended, my guilt weighed more heavily, and I questioned my mind and my motives. But that white specter of the afterlife was everywhere. Reflected in the mirror behind the bar. Clinging to the ceiling, like it was part of the rising smoke haze. Sitting right there at the table with us, grinning, while we ate in sullen silence. I closed my eyes. I whispered a protective prayer. There was no room for misgivings anymore.

There was simply a job that had to be done.

It was that or be forever haunted.

Seth chewed loudly, ravaged his lunch like a starving animal. His knife and fork clattered against his tin plate. Blood flowed red from the meat. Cowboys beat their hands against the bar, called out to a man named Brick who was pouring drinks, demanding another round. A pair of women, seated at a table in the corner, smoked cigars and shrieked with laughter. Despite the cool wind that had ushered in the storm, the room was hot as a furnace, and I began to sweat through my already-sodden clothes. I wished in that moment to be in any other saloon, in any other town, with any other people than these. But mine was a situation of my own making, and deep in my soul, I knew these were the only sort of companions I deserved.

Aubrey went to the bar. Returned with a whiskey bottle.

We went to work on that bottle like it was our job.

"This is a fine steak," said Seth.

"The street's full of cows," said Aubrey. "I imagine the meat's fresh."

"They got cows in St. Louis," he said. "Still never had a steak taste that good."

"You're just hungry is all."

"You don't like yours?"

"Yes, it's fine enough."

"You can't enjoy nothing, can you?" Seth's face darkened, his good humor laid low by his brother's indifference.

Aubrey scowled. "I can get on my knees and worship the god damn steak if that's what you want."

"I swear," said Seth, "if someone gave you a bag of gold, you'd complain the bag wasn't fancy enough. I can't understand why you'd rather be miserable all the time. Look at us. Out here at the edge of civilization, money weighing down our pockets. This is high adventure. You need to soak in all this fresh air, Aubrey. You need to *live*."

"Right now," said Aubrey, "life is uncomfortable and wet. Half of me wishes I'd stayed home."

"And the other half of you's drunk," said Seth.

"No argument."

Seth pointed his fork at me. "I don't mean to offend, Doc, but you're the reason he's behaving like this."

"How am I to blame?" I asked.

"There's a cloud follows you around. Again, no offense."

"Hard not to be offended." I spoke with a smile, for we both knew Seth was telling the truth.

Seth sawed off another bite of steak, chewed his way though it while he spoke. "Aubrey here always walks in sunshine. You get my meaning? And now we've followed you out here and he's moping around like someone killed his dog. I'll speak plainly, Doc. I like you. I don't believe you intend to be a bad person. But you are a poor influence. Once this job is done, I'm taking Aubrey and we're leaving you behind in a hurry. Whatever gloom follows you around has latched on to my brother too. I fear he's become enchanted by your witchery. I know you've not explained yourself in full to us, and that's fine, but I'm an observant man. Your drunken confessions and your whispered spells and the curious notions in your leather bag have not gone unnoticed by me."

Whatever humor I'd found in Seth's petulant manner vanished, and the smile I offered him was no longer the friendly kind. "Well, that's a fine thing. A killer questioning my morality."

"Better a killer than a witch, I reckon."

"I'm not a witch."

"Are you not?"

"I will admit to an unorthodox sort of spritualty, but I would not call myself a witch."

"It doesn't matter what you call yourself," said Seth. "My brother has fallen under a dark spell, just the same."

"Seth, I can tend to myself," said Aubrey.

"I don't believe you can," said Seth. "Not when it comes to her."

Aubrey threw back a long swallow from our shared bottle, grimaced like he was chewing on glass. "I know all about Dr. Coldbridge and what's expected here. She may not have explained herself to you, but I enjoy a full understanding of matters. Don't presume to be my keeper, and don't talk to me as if I'm a fool with no idea of what we're riding into. *You're* the one followed *me* on this journey. The doctor explained to me back in St. Louis the reason her husband requires killing, in no uncertain terms, and not a little about the bloody circumstances that caused their estrangement. If you believe Dr. Coldbridge and her *rituals* are the source of my ills, then you've not studied me closely enough in our forty-one years of life. I am capable of my own dark moods with no outside assistance; any black clouds that pass over me, you can be sure I summoned them myself."

"So, you're keeping secrets from me?" said Seth.

"Don't look at it like that," said Aubrey. "More like I have provided you just enough information to proceed without the burden of anxiety."

"Go to Hell, Aubrey."

"Trying hard as I can."

Seth shoved his chair back from the table. Donned his hat and made a show of tucking in his shirttail. "Seems you and the good doctor have this whole mess figured, then. Since I'm not necessary to the proceedings, I'll leave you to it. See if I can't find friendlier companionship."

Seth marched through the swinging doors of the Silver Ace, headed back out into the constant afternoon rain.

I'd never seen the brothers cross with one another. Good-natured ribbing, maybe a few gruff remarks, but nothing that revealed a rift. Again, I considered what wild cards both men were, and how little I understood them. Our first meeting had been happenstance. A night of overindulgence and loud boasting that had drawn me into their circle and given me the idea that they might be hard enough characters for the job I so desperately needed done. That whiskey hall in St. Louis had been hot and crowded, and Seth had left with a couple friends to find some place quieter to play cards. Aubrey and I stayed, went through a few more bottles. Carried on until night spilled over into morning. So entangled with one another that when I suggested he help me kill my husband, he just grinned and asked how much I was paying. All night he'd gone on about the places they'd robbed and the people he'd killed back in his wilder days, and it was only now that I began to realize he could have sold me any story that night, and I'd have bought it. There was nothing verifiable about the Dawson brothers. Not their names. Not their histories. Not even their provenance as killers. Only Aubrey's word offered any supporting evidence that they were fit for this kind of work.

But it was too late for second guesses.

We'd find out soon, one way or another.

"You didn't tell him about Frank?" I asked.

"I told him we traveled here to kill him."

"But not the fact that he's *difficult* to kill."

"Might be I'm the one risking your offense now, but I just don't believe you. There's no man can survive a properly placed bullet. I'm happy to take your money for a job you could probably do yourself with a lady's pistol, but there's no reason to get Seth wound up. He's more credulous than me, and matters like ghosts and black magic and walking dead men cause him to become overwrought. So, just a simple job here, as far as he's concerned. And I have listened to your talk of spells and rituals, and maybe you think Frank died up there in Montana and you somehow breathed life back into his lungs. Maybe you really *believe* it. But understand this. I think every word of that story is bullshit, and tomorrow I'll prove it by killing that bastard deader than General Custer."

Aubrey kept that cool smile on his face the whole time he spoke, but I realized Seth was right. Aubrey was fading. Maybe it was the way the rain had dulled his finery, giving him a disheveled look for the first time. Casting him as a soul with too much weight on his shoulders. His eyes were glassy, and his face was drawn, but he was still handsome as the devil. Moreso than ever, maybe. I found myself looking for reasons to hate him, but I understood what it meant to accidentally walk down the wrong path in life, and find yourself stranded in the wilderness forever. I reached across the table, put my hand on top of his, and left it there. His gaze had begun to drift off, maybe wishing he could take back some of what he said, but my gesture shocked him back into the moment.

"I appreciate your candor," I said, though we both knew I'd rather him have kept quiet. Neither one of us was overfond of the truth.

"Like Seth said, no offense intended."

"I can't imagine what you gentlemen would have to say to me if you actually intended offense."

"We can be poor companions."

"I had noticed that. Don't worry. We understand one another

better now, I think. And there might be a few things about you I don't believe either."

"Such as?"

"Are you really a cold-blooded killer?"

"Indeed I am."

"You've offered no proof of that."

"There are card cheats and fidgety bank tellers who would testify to my truth, but they're all currently occupying pine coffins."

"So very convenient," I said. "You wouldn't kill *me*, would you?"

"Not unless you really needed killing," he said. "I've grown fond of you."

"Well, that's a relief then."

I hoped the Dawson brothers were as fierce and deadly as they claimed. Capable of making a quick end of things with nothing more than bullets and a willingness to murder for money. But even if they were, it was possible their competence as killers would not factor into what I was planning. If bullets wouldn't do the trick, and I had reason to believe they might not, I would need the men to subdue Frank while I worked a ritual. To keep him still and bound long enough for me to withdraw his soul from his body again, and send it to the afterlife where it should have gone when he died, so many years ago.

Frank was a monster, but I couldn't blame him for it. That was my fault entirely.

I should have left him dead.

Aubrey and I sat together drinking until the sun fell, and the Silver Ace grew even more raucous. My head pounded, and my stomach grew sick. Blood thundered in my temples. My mouth was dry, and my ears rang, and every voice in the room boomed like thunder. The rain continued in earnest, and the place grew hot with life. Redolent of sweat. Every eye seemed to look our way, black and empty, like death was keeping a close watch on our endeavors. The weight of my surroundings became unbearable. We arranged for rooms upstairs, and when I finally pushed away from the table to seek out a bed, my deathly companion followed, sheathed in white smoke and wispy at the edges, grinning and hungry and eager to terrorize me through every second of my life. It followed in my wake, up the stairs, into my room. Lingered like a mist against the ceiling as I lay in bed, so that when I closed my eyes, I could still feel the afterlife gazing down at me, expectantly.

I wondered if it would take me while I slept.

Wondered if that would be such a bad thing.

I felt cold and lonely and desperate.

And when Aubrey knocked at my door, deep in the night, I let him in without hesitation.

Acolytes of the Three Rose Temple
From Fort Ellis into the Wilderness, Montana Territory
Autumn 1879

THREE DAYS AFTER FRANK RODE OUT in search of bandits, Corporal Levi's leg had improved dramatically. The medicines I'd applied, and my surreptitious calling to spirits for their aid had reversed the course of his infection and rendered him awake and in full possession of his parts. Dr. Prosper failed to hide his disappointment. The bone saw, for now, would continue to gather dust.

I occupied my time with patient care, and tried to ignore the pervasive sense of dread I'd developed since Frank left the fort. It wasn't easy. I kept imagining his lifeless body being rolled through the gates on a wagon. Pierced with arrows. Filled with bullet holes. Broken and bloody. When I slept, my dreams added colors and dimensions to my fears that were beyond even my waking terrors. I had learned long ago to listen to my mind when it whispered to me, and to heed messages from my dreams. But I strove to leaven these concerns with a dose of reality. Not every fear is valid. Not every nightmare a presentiment of things to come. And I was able to convince myself of this, until the moment Falling Bird strode into the hospital, limping and lathered in blood.

For a moment I thought he might be a mirage, a waking nightmare that escaped my mind.

Falling Bird could not be here. Not alone.

He wore a horrified expression, and his body shook as if electrified.

"What's happened?" I asked the question, already certain I knew the answer. My hands began to examine him, working on instinct, independent of my racing mind.

"It's not my blood," he said. "Not most of it."

"What happened?" I asked again.

"I came here, straight to you," he said. "I'm sorry."

"Sorry for what?"

"They're all dead," he said. "All except me."

"Not Frank, though."

Falling Bird grimaced. Tried to hug me, but I flinched.

"You're saying Frank's dead?"

He nodded. "I came straight to tell you."

My hands stopped moving. My fingers clutched at his buffalo coat; the hide was matted with blood. Falling Bird smelled like death, like horses ridden too hard. He was a creature of sweat and dirt and terror. I tightened my grip on his coat, afraid I'd tumble to the ground beneath the weight of his revelations. *Frank was dead.* When Falling Bird spoke again, his voice came to me from a dream. I couldn't hear every word, but he made plain the reality of what had happened. *Frank was dead.* The patrol had allowed itself to be caught out in a low valley. A band of Sioux rode down on them with carbines and arrows. But not before unleashing an artillery barrage from a pair of cannons, liberated from the Army in some past battle. *Frank was dead.* Falling Bird believed the attack on the boy in the buckboard was only meant to lure a patrol into the trap, and this would certainly not be the first time that had happened during the protracted conflict between the Plains Indians and the Army. There had been at least forty of them. Falling Bird killed three, but the patrol was overwhelmed, and he'd fled the valley, the last Fort Ellis man alive. *Frank was dead.* The Sioux had been content to gather the patrol's horses and supplies, and had not given chase as Falling Bird raced back to the fort.

Frank was dead.

"I can help him," I said.

"Dr. Coldbridge, I told you, he's dead."

"That doesn't matter. I can help him."

"I believe you're in a state of shock."

"You're not wrong, but the fact remains, I can help."

"I don't think you understand me."

"Can you tell me where to find him?"

Falling Bird shook his head. "You can't ride to him. His killers have likely fled, but that is not a certainty. My return has not gone unnoticed. Men are being mustered. Several hundred, I would imagine. If those who attacked us are foolish enough to be ranging about, they will face a furious response."

"Revenge is fine," I said. "But I mean to go to my husband."

"I assure you he's gone," said Falling Bird. "His body is broken beyond saving."

"Where is he?"

"Dr. Coldbridge, there's no—"

"Tell me where he is!"

I hadn't meant to scream, but my fury escaped, nonetheless. Corporal Levi woke from a sound sleep; he wriggled up into a sitting position in his bed, groaning but in full possession of his faculties. The vomiting patient never opened his eyes; he stayed lying on one side with a bucket nearby. My hands still held Falling Bird's coat, like losing hold of him would be losing hold of reality. Like if they released their grip, the rest of me would fade from this world to join my mother, my father, my husband, in the afterlife.

Frank was dead.

"I'm sorry," I said.

"There's no reason for sorry," said Falling Bird.

"I understand what you're saying," I said. "Believe that I do. But I am riding out to get Frank. Whether you tell me where to find him or not, I'm going. If I must wander the plains until chance delivers him to me, I'm going. Do you understand what *I'm* saying?"

"I can tell you where he is, but you can't go alone."

"Then you'll take me to him?"

"It's not safe, Dr. Coldbridge."

"I haven't a care about safe."

"We followed signs for quite a way before they sprung the trap. Many miles. I rode a full day and night to get back here, pushing my horse hard the whole way," he said. "And we'll have to sleep rough. It will be more of a hardship than you're accustomed to."

"You think I've never slept on the ground, under the open sky? I've done so covered in blood and bile and reeking of death. This is not my first posting. My time here has not been limited to the stifling confines of this hospital. I've engaged in plenty of field medicine. I've seen the worst things a person can see. Sleeping outdoors is the least of my concerns."

"You will not be dissuaded?"

"I will not."

"Then I suppose I'll take you," he said. "If only to keep you alive. Have you time to administer some medical care, or would you prefer I ride back out to my death on just one good leg?"

I resumed my examination, and discovered that a bullet had pierced Falling Bird's forearm, and an arrow had found the meat of his thigh. The bullet passed through clean, and he'd managed to get the arrow out somewhere between the valley where they'd been attacked and Fort Ellis. I gathered it was not the first time he'd been touched by an arrow, and he'd already cleaned and wrapped the wound. There appeared no risk of infection, but I redressed both his leg and his arm, and applied a bit of my poultice for good measure.

Guilt pained me. The fact that I'd implored Falling Bird to follow me in this condition was selfish and unkind. But Montana was huge, and I didn't truly believe I could find Frank without him.

"You are a good friend to ride with me," I said.

"Have I any choice?"

"I don't suppose I've left you one."

"You plan to bring his body back?"

"I plan to bring *Frank* back."

Falling Bird went silent, determined now that his arguments would find no willing ear. He watched me, eyes flooded with grief, as I finished tending his wounds. I wondered how much a fool he thought me to be. Of course, he could not know what I intended. Not even Frank was privy to my esoteric studies, and my initiation into what my mentor called the *western mysteries*.

Even I had no idea what the outcome would be. The ritual I intended was one I'd never tried. One I'd been cautioned against.

But I didn't care.

Frank was dead.

Falling Bird secured a flatbed wagon and a team of horses from the corral quartermaster. Enough rations and water to last us a week if necessary. I retrieved my bag. Ensured it contained my black book, and the ritual elements required.

Our preparations complete, we left the safety of the fort.

I meant to bring my husband back, dead or alive.

———————

Perhaps those who've never lost someone close to them would question my mind and my motives as we hurried the wagon team across the plains and over the foothills. Perhaps they would be wholly unfamiliar with the powerful hold desperation can have on a person. But I hope they could forgive me for believing my peculiar talents might offer solutions unavailable to others. Grief creates a miasma of frantic thoughts and poor choices. Grief abandons us to our basest instincts. And while my conscious mind understood, even in that moment, what a burden my actions might put on my soul, I gave no thought to abandoning my course. No thought to facing my misery and allowing it to speak an end to the life I believed I deserved.

I was a god damn fool.

Falling Bird held the reins. Guided us toward the last place my husband ever drew breath. I bounced in the seat beside him, studying my black book and working to convince myself I had the strength and knowledge for what had to be done.

"What are you planning to do?" he asked.

His words broke my concentration, my *preparation*, and when I responded, it was with more fire than I intended.

"I have told you what I plan to do," I said. "Let me be plain so I don't have to answer you again. I'm going to find my husband's body, repair it as best I can, and then bring him back to life. I'm going to find his soul on the astral plane, or at least what's left of it, and summon it back into his body. How may I further clarify this for you?"

Falling Bird shook his head. "I understand you're grieving, but this is foolishness."

"You're a Crow," I said. "Don't you believe in spirits?"

"Aren't I an ignorant savage, you mean."

"No, that's not what I meant."

"Oh, I think you meant it a little."

"I'm sorry, I just didn't think you'd doubt me."

"You didn't think I'd doubt your ability to bring a man back from the dead?"

Of course, he was right. Why should he believe me? Why should anyone?

"I've seen odd things," he said. "Colored stars that move across the night sky like flocks of birds. Ghosts, maybe. Spirits on horseback, navigating the landscape in the early morning hours. And the old people talk about stalking shadows and men who shapeshift into monsters. Strangeness inhabited this country before people came here, and I believe it touches our lives in ways we can perceive, and ways we can't. But this thing you're talking about? Dead is dead, Catherine. It's an unwavering truth. Might be part of Frank's spirit wanders this place now, unable to move on. And if you believe that to be so, I'm sorry. But he belongs to the afterlife now. There's no coming back from death."

"Maybe you're right," I said. "But I mean to try."

"You truly believe you can do this?"

"Oh, yes."

"And if you're wrong?"

"Then we'll at least have a body to bury."

Falling Bird had no faith in me, but I couldn't hold that against him. To any rational person, what I proposed was absurd. I'd have reacted with the same degree of skepticism, probably more, had I not spent years learning a new sort of spirituality, and honing my desires and my will into reality. I practiced divination and trance meditation. I could unlock my spirit from my body and travel beyond the material world. I could beseech angels and devils and other ethereal spirits to work in the world on my behalf. All this knowledge resided in my secret heart, and enlivened my soul.

When I spoke my intentions, I expected those words to yield results. And though I'd never seen anyone come back from the dead, I believed it could be done.

No matter how I'd been counseled against trying.

No matter the warnings.

I'd acquired my occult knowledge in medical school, though certainly not as part of the ordinary curriculum. My parents were rather progressive, proud to send me to the Woman's Medical College of Pennsylvania. Never questioning my desire to be a doctor, or suggesting that marriage to any of the numerous eligible bachelors who swarmed around me in Philadelphia might result in an easier life. My parents understood me, and they put the full force of their support behind my goals. I cannot remember at what age I decided to be a doctor, or the circumstances that informed that desire; it was ever present, like I'd been born a doctor, and spent my youth waiting to become the person I already was.

School was easy. I have never had difficulty learning. Friendships flourished and my instructors often remarked on my tenacity and my quick mind. I recall that first year in school with a fondness that I've rarely felt for anything since. My second year, I became friends with Louisa Jupiter. While only a month older than me, Louisa was far more mature, able to navigate the world and its mysteries in ways I had not yet discovered. She too excelled in her studies, yet it was her extracurricular activities that formed the core of her being, as if medicine was a fine vocation, but not the thing that would truly define her. Louisa was pledged to an organization called the Three Rose Temple, and though the purview of this strange group was *literal magick*, a prospect I found frankly absurd, she was never reluctant to speak of it. In fact, Louisa was so earnest about her involvement and the positive changes the Three Rose Temple had affected in her life, that I accepted her invitation to attend one of their gatherings, if for no other reason than to prove how smart I was by debunking whatever nonsense they had on offer.

It was not so simple as that.

Magick was real, if not exactly how I imagined it.

At first, pledging the Three Rose Temple seemed nothing more than an embarrassing procession of flowing robes and ridiculous costumes. Ceremonial daggers and choking incense and black candles throwing heavy shadows across indecipherable chalk-drawn symbols. Every ceremony reeked of playacting. Every chant and prayer sounded like ineffectual nonsense. Then patterns began to emerge. Difficult ideas took root in my mind. My will began to materialize into actual reality. Things about myself that I never understood suddenly became transparent. Things I desired in the world were suddenly attainable. The Three Rose Temple did not change me, so much as it revealed the person I'd always been.

The organization accepted me. Fostered me.

I learned that magick was one of the rare disciplines wherein men and women were allowed to begin and advance in their studies on equal footing. Every possibility opened for me.

Louisa and I became fast friends. And after a time, more than friends. I fell in love with her mind and her beauty and the way she moved in the world. Never had I been so captivated by another person, and under other circumstances, we might have lived out our lives together, our love and our partnership unbreakable. I'd have never gone West. Never met Frank. And as much as I came to love him immensely, there were days that my memories ran back to Louisa, and I wondered why I'd let matters of life and death intervene to tear us apart.

"Have you done this before?" asked Falling Bird.

"Bring someone back?"

"Yes."

"No, I haven't. But I know it will work."

I didn't really *know* it would work, but I *believed* it would work. And belief was far more important to successful magick than certainty.

"What is that, your spell book?"

Falling Bird pointed at the black book I still clutched tight in my hands. It was an unremarkable leather journal that Louisa had gifted me long ago. I'd used it to copy down every rite and ritual I learned, and many I'd never tried.

"I suppose that's an accurate enough description."

"Might want to cover it up, so it won't get ruined."

As if his words summoned the rain, fat drops began to strike the wagon and our heads. I tucked the book under my coat. Black clouds rode the wind, chased off the afternoon sun. The rain was cold, and the wind cut through us like a cavalry saber. Lightning traversed the horizon, and thunder sounded, just a few heartbeats later. I imagined Frank, lying dead on the ground, icy rain splashing against his wide opened eyes and drenching his bloody uniform. His mouth agape, filled with water that overflowed down his cheeks. A silent scream was lodged in his throat. He was all but begging me to hurry. To help him return before the rest of him dissolved into dust. I willed the team of horses to work harder, pull faster, calm themselves enough to proceed apace through the suddenly slapping rain and riotous thunder.

"I don't suppose you'll allow us to seek shelter?" asked Falling Bird.

"We don't have time for delay."

"We'll be no help if we're struck by lightning."

"Please, keep going."

Falling Bird made no move to slow the team. We rumbled across the uneven terrain, bouncing and sore but making steady progress. After a time, the rainfall slowed, but lightning continued to lance across the sky.

"You're kind to take me to him," I said. "Can I repay you by at least trying to explain what I believe, and why I'm doing this?"

Falling Bird didn't respond, but he didn't object. I took it as a sign to proceed.

"There's a world apart from this one, a place where we store all we are and all we could be. I used to study with an organization of Hermetic mages, and they taught me about it. I know it sounds crazy, but just listen. This world apart, they called it the astral plane. There was one old man in the group who fancied himself a poet. He called it the *underside of existence*. It really doesn't matter. The astral plane is an actual place. Some even consider it the realm of death, though I'm not sure. The astral plane is where we send all the energy we release into the world, good or bad, and it waits for us there, until we need it. So, if you are a great marksman, you store some of that energy there. If you have brown eyes and long hair, a bit of that memory is stored there as well. All of you. Everything. There are ways to separate from your physical body, unmoor your soul to go adventuring. And you can slip into this astral version of yourself like a well-tailored suit. Is any of this making sense?"

Falling Bird whistled at the horses, snapped the reins, but otherwise kept quiet.

"Well, all this energy remains there, waiting for us. Until we need it? Some say when we die, we put on that other self for good, and venture off to whatever awaits us next, full of life experiences. Sometimes, if people aren't ready, they might inhabit their other self, but remain close to the material world. Unwilling to let go. I believe that's what we mean when we call something a ghost.

"I believe Frank's not ready. I believe I can gather up his soul and his energy and put it right back inside his corpse. See him draw breath and see him open his eyes and smile at me again. I have a ritual in this book. If it works as written, we can bring him back."

Falling Bird wasn't laughing at me. That much was a comfort. Finally, he turned his eyes to mine, and I could see he had at least listened. He'd at least taken what I said to heart, whether he believed me or not.

"I hear a lot of *ifs* and *believes* in what you say," he said. "I'm not a stranger to the ways we can fool ourselves into seeing the world how we want it to be. Are you sure you aren't doing the same?"

"No, I suppose I'm not."

"Why do you think his soul remains in this place?"

"He loves me. He knows I love him. He wouldn't want to leave me."

"Everyone loves *someone*," he said. "Most of them die when they're supposed to."

"I know that."

"Even if what you say is true, putting his soul back in his body is unnatural. I can't imagine these spirits of yours won't demand a price for something like that."

"Oh, there's always a price," I said. "You have to be willing to pay it, and I am."

"You're sure of that?"

"No alternative exists, save for living the rest of my life without Frank. The universe may name its price. I'll pay it gladly."

"I still don't believe you can do this thing," he said.

"I don't expect you to."

I held my black book against my chest, as if I might absorb every bit of power and love and hope I'd invested in those pages. I thought about my parents, coughing up their lungs. I thought of Frank, terrified as his killers rained arrows down on him. All I'd wanted was to stall the creeping death that stalked my parents, but my magick had not been adequate for the task.

When they died, something snapped inside me.

The Three Rose Temple had a large library of esoteric volumes; books with transparent vellum pages, some illuminated by rogue priests with belief systems that got them hung, a few inked in blood in languages long dead. I examined them all. Noted down anything of interest in my black book. And then I discovered a slim red book written in German with a title that translated quite simply to *Defeating Death*, and it contained everything I'd hoped to find.

A ritual for summoning life back into dead bodies.

I thought Louisa would be happy for me. I assumed she'd throw her full support behind what I intended. Instead, she argued. Demanded I pursue another course. Went so far as to hide my black book, for a time, along with the original German volume.

She'd never lost anyone. How could she understand that sort of desperation?

Eventually she relented, though she assured me there were some rituals that should never be tried. But by then, it was too late. My parents were gone. Their souls had fled beyond my reach.

Louisa tried to console me.

I never forgave her.

Death had taken my parents when I might have done something to stop it.

I wouldn't let it have Frank too.

Bloody Mythmaking
The Fairgrounds, Fort Worth, Texas
Spring 1905

THE RAIN FLED OVERNIGHT, leaving Fort Worth sunny and warm, and when I joined the Dawson brothers for breakfast, there remained no trace of the previous night's animosity. Seth seemed in high spirits, and Aubrey wore a serene smile. The brothers might disagree, but it appeared they could not stay cross with one another for long. Brick, the bartender, directed us to a dress shop and a haberdashery, and I outfitted the three of us in dry clothes, appropriate for our trip to the Wild West Revue. I bought a blue French silk dress with broad shoulders and prominent bustle, and a matching parasol to shield my tired eyes from the afternoon sun. Seth chose a dull brown suit, and talked himself into a top hat that sat uneasy on his head, leaning forward like a drunkard, ready to topple to the ground at any moment. Aubrey's suit was finer, an olive-green check cutaway, and his stiff shirt collar wrapped tight as a hangman's noose around his neck. He chose a wide-brimmed Stetson with a pale silk band, and I judged us fit for a day at the fairgrounds, if a bit overdressed for the business that would follow.

Fort Worth teemed with humanity; the storm had kept everyone home the day before, and now they sought sun and entertainment and commerce. More cattle than people moved through the streets, presumably on their way to a train car, and eventually a slaughterhouse. We were perhaps not entirely unlike them, marching toward a fate that none of us would have chosen, but unable to extricate ourselves from binding circumstances.

Cowboy Dan's Wild West Revue was being held in a field not far from the Fort Worth train station, and the torrent of rain left everything a sloppy mess. We passed by a scattering of wind-tossed tents that housed the performers and the men who managed the show, breathing in the cool air that lingered in the wake of the storm. One of the tents surely belonged to Frank, but I was not ready to face him yet. I wanted to see him in person, first. Wanted to watch the show, and find out if the advertisements were true.

The place was alive and in motion. Food cooked on massive grills, and horses whickered. Laughter rose bright and sharp from somewhere across camp. An older-style stagecoach with THE GOLDEN GULCH stenciled in ornate letters on the side appeared stuck in the mud, and several men wedged boards under the wheels, working to free it. A couple of arrows stuck out from the back of it, presumably remnants of an earlier performance. Cowboys herded a dozen head of buffalo into the fenced-in parade grounds, so they could roam in the shadows of a hastily erected grandstand. Pennants flapped from the upper reaches of that structure, and the sky ran blue and endless overhead. I'd read in the papers that Cowboy Dan employed close to two hundred souls: dancing cowgirls, trick riders, sharpshooters, actors, orators, outlaws, Indians, and cavalry riders, along with the cooks and carpenters and teamsters that kept the whole operation moving from city to city.

All of them, and Frank, of course.

The performance was scheduled for midafternoon, so we bought three tickets, milled about in the growing crowd until ushers unlocked the gate, and led us to our seats in the grandstand. We settled in. Listened as a brass band began to play "Home on the Range."

I closed my eyes, whispered a prayer to the spirits, assured in my plans, and certain we were about to witness the last ever performance by the sideshow monster they called the Unkillable Frank Lightning.

Cowboy Dan rode out on a fleet white horse to great fanfare, waving his hat over his head, and Seth hooted as if the angels had come to deliver him to glory. The old man was a dime novel come to life, sliding from his saddle smooth as spilled whiskey. He wore a deerskin coat with fringe beneath the arms, giving the impression he might take flight as he waved his hands at the crowd. He drew twin pistols, fired them at the air, and the crowd provided a robust response. Seth seemed ready to come unglued from his seat, maybe see if he could get hired on, but if Aubrey was impressed by the man's celebrity, he hid it behind his impenetrable smirk.

Cowboy Dan issued a long oration on the taming of the West, and particularly his vital part in the task. To hear Dan tell it, he'd spent time as a Pinkerton in Missouri, robbed trains in Kansas, and dodged Pawnee arrows while riding for the Pony Express. Dan fought against, and alongside, seemingly every Indian tribe from the Rio Grande to the Canadian border. He traded rifle shots with Comanches at Adobe Walls, and rode with Billy the Kid during the Lincoln County War. In his clear, stentorian voice, he assured the crowd that Billy was alive and well and working at a saloon in California, and there never had been born a friendlier killer. He regaled us with tales of his time as a lawman in Dodge City and Deadwood, and of a high-stakes poker game against Doc Holliday himself. He urged some of the crowd to tears with the story of a Sioux woman he'd romanced in the Dakotas, who'd died of smallpox. Theirs had been a great love, and her ghost, so he claimed, haunted him to that very day.

It was all so preposterous. A tangle of exaggerations and outright lies. But the crowd didn't care. They embraced the tall tales.

Truth was a worthless commodity when fiction was so much more exciting.

"Sounds like Cowboy Dan gets around," said Aubrey.

"He's a boastful fool," I said.

"You believe he scouted with Kit Carson?" asked Seth.

"No, I do not," I said.

"Doesn't matter if he did, or if he didn't," said Aubrey. "It makes for a good story."

"Makes for good lies, more like."

"No, he's not a liar. He's a showman."

"Two sides of the same coin," I said.

Eventually Dan welcomed the performers. Horses danced and buffaloes lumbered. Riders raced one another with flags billowing behind them and gunshots ringing in the air. Longhorns thrashed about as a host of cowboys herded them in ever-widening circles—a cattle drive, in miniature. Dan introduced the lead rider as Thirsty Picket, King of the Cowboys, and Thirsty, an old man who looked weathered as the steep side of a mountain, doffed his hat, and waved it at the crowd. According to Dan, Thirsty had been a top hand for several famous ranching outfits. He certainly looked the part, but I was disinclined to take Dan at his word.

When the animals cleared out, the sharpshooters commenced. A woman named Mabel Bones entered the fairground on horseback, at a full gallop, and before she reached the far end of the arena, she shattered ten glass bottles with bullets from her Winchester repeating rifle. Mabel never slowed, just sat in that saddle like it was an easy chair in her grandmother's parlor, took aim at the bottles standing along the back fence line, and brought them down in quick succession. With that same rifle, she hit targets blindfolded, shooting backward over her shoulder while aiming with a mirror, and then hopped back on her horse and repeated her ride in reverse, murdering ten more bottles on her way out. The crowd loved it, and I will admit that her skill was enough to stir something inside me too. The proceedings might have the slick veneer of fakery to them, but it was obvious Mabel's talents were genuine.

A boy no older than fifteen marched out next. He was skinny and sun reddened, wearing a wide-brimmed hat, denim pants, and down at heel boots. Cowboy Dan introduced him as the Hurricane Kid. Holstered pistols rode low on both hips. The boy had haunted eyes, like he was looking through the crowd, and not at us. He gave a perfunctory tip of his hat, then lurched into action. I have never seen a person draw a pistol so fast. Never before that day, and never since. The Kid shot from the hip. His target was a tin windmill, with small flat blades designed to spin the whole thing on the axle when struck. He emptied all six shots from one heavy revolver, and every one hit. Then the second gun was in his hand, like he'd called it from thin air, and all six of those shots struck home as well. The *ping, ping, ping* of bullets striking the target came so fast, I could barely register the silence between them.

Aubrey watched the performance with a cool, appraising stare, and I couldn't help but prod him.

"You've said you're fond of testing yourself against all comers, when it comes to your pistol," I said. "You may want to control your urges in that regard, while the Hurricane Kid is in close proximity."

"Oh, I believe I could take him."

"He's fast."

"Not fast as me."

During our brief exchange, the Hurricane Kid had reloaded both pistols and pinged the target with all twelve bullets.

Twice.

"Your confidence rivals that of Cowboy Dan."

"Cowboy Dan can go hang, and so can that boy." Aubrey was still smiling, but a black mood lurked in the corners of his eyes. "There's a difference between shooting metal ducks and figuring which rib you need to put a bullet through to strike a man's heart. That boy's not old enough to have blood that cold."

"Hardness can settle in a soul at any age. Desperate circumstances don't discriminate. I was quite young myself when I gave up on the world."

More than the boy's haunted expression unsettled me. There was a heaviness about him, like he changed the atmosphere when he strode into the arena. The crowd didn't seem to notice; they cheered with every crack of the pistol. But I had learned to trust what the world was telling me, and my magickal studies had opened my eyes to auras, a sort of energy that surrounds people like a second skin, pulsing and writhing and colorful. Though certainly not infallible, auras could allow me to gauge a person's mood, or their intentions. Seth, in that moment, was colored by a red and lively light, as he laughed and clapped and cheered the boy's talents. Aubrey was a sullen, sickly green. He studied the boy's movements, taking mental notes. The Hurricane Kid continued his shooting, mustang fast, yet workmanlike. And his aura was gray and fleeting, like chimney smoke disappearing into the clouds. I'd never seen anything like it on a living person, and I was frankly baffled.

The Hurricane Kid was certainly *in* this world, but I could not be certain he was entirely *of* it.

I had encountered many strange things in my studies, but the young shootist was a mystery.

"You have not given up on the world." Aubrey's words shook my concentration, and the auras faded from sight.

"Oh, you've read me wrong, sir."

"I don't believe I have."

"Please then, do tell me all the things I don't know about myself."

"If you were truly finished with this world, you would not be so set on this errand," said Aubrey. "There are far more comfortable locales to drink oneself to death."

As if to demonstrate the truth of what he said, Aubrey shifted uncomfortably in his seat, then took a drink from his ever-present flask. He didn't have to offer it to me afterward. I held out my hand, took it and drank.

"I owe the world a debt, that's all."

"Nobody owes the world anything," he said. "We must simply survive as best we can."

"Bold words from a killer."

"Some of us survive better than others."

"I'm not judging you," I said. "We're both killers, in our own way."

"Perhaps that's why I've grown so fond of you."

"Don't get too attached," I said. "Once this deed is done, I will commence to drinking myself to death in earnest. You may watch if you like, and perhaps will come to understand me better."

"Your despair is contagious."

"I believe that's what I was telling you last night," said Seth.

"Be quiet, Seth," said Aubrey. "Watch the show."

"My despair is well-earned," I said. "I used to want to understand everything about the universe, so I turned all my considerable talents to that learning. My efforts were largely rewarded with answers. Problem is, I had not expected the answers to be so unsatisfactory."

"We must live in the world as it is, not the world as we wish it was," said Aubrey.

"Where did you read that mawkish homily?"

"It was something our mother used to say."

"Before she died," said Seth.

"I assumed that much," I said. "She doesn't sound the sort to deliver missives from the grave."

"I don't believe she'd like you much," said Seth.

"I'm confident she *would not*," I said.

The *Wild West Revue* carried on while we talked, and I found myself unable to focus on the parade of riders and ropers and costumed actors. I didn't return Aubrey's flask; instead, I drank it dry, and let the heat of the day settle around me in a comfortable haze. Horses whickered and rifles cracked, but it all passed before me like a dream that I could barely remember after waking. At some point, I realized Aubrey was holding my hand, giving it a squeeze, and I looked up to see Cowboy Dan in the center of the arena once more. His voice seemed louder than ever, and his aura was a frantic mix of orange and red. He announced the climax of the show, suggested none of us were prepared for the coming spectacle.

He urged us to sturdy ourselves for a riot of violence and human perseverance. A furious melody of rifle cracks and whistling arrows. A celebration of gun smoke and blood.

A paean to the *American fighting spirit*.

Then a giant stalked into the arena.

He waved his hat, and the crowd roared.

And for the first time in over twenty-five years, I laid eyes on my dead husband.

The crowd cheered as the Unkillable Frank Lightning strode across the arena. He moved like a great lumbering bear, slow as sunrise but just as inevitable. He kept waving his hat in the air, revealing the angry scars on his head, evidence of where he'd been scalped, and where I'd pieced him together again. Those same scars ran down behind his ears and across this throat, and though he was covered entirely in buckskins, I knew the scars drew a roadmap across his chest, his back, his arms, and every part of him. His skin was the palest green, evidence of the corrupting influence of death that had not entirely left him. Frank managed a smile with his piecemeal face, and terror chased up my spine. Last time I'd seen that face, it had been covered in blood and howling like a hurricane.

Indians on painted horses rode into the arena and massed along the far wall, several wearing long headdresses, others lifting feathered lances and waving tomahawks in a vaguely threatening fashion. Based on their dress, I made them as a mix of Kiowa, Apache, and a few Comanches. But Cowboy Dan continued to show little regard for the truth. By the time he finished introducing them, half the crowd believed these were *the very same Pawnee warriors* who had attacked while he was guarding the *Golden Gulch* stagecoach deep in the Kansas heartland. It had been a fine battle, and Cowboy Dan had not only taken several arrows to his back, but narrowly avoided a scalping. He'd prevailed, of course, and chased away the last of the raiders with a barrage of shots from his trusty Sharps rifle. My brain enumerated the historical inaccuracies and multiplied that number by the outright lies and finally concluded there was no way to truly understand Cowboy Dan. Rather, one must simply accept the questionable mathematics of his life story.

· Frank stood next to Cowboy Dan as the *Golden Gulch* stage rolled into the arena, wheels throwing up water as they moved through puddles left by the overnight rain. The old cowboy, Thirsty Picket, drove the stage, weathered hands on the reins, guiding a team of four horses. This arrival elicited yelling and mock animosity from the Indian actors. One of them fired a warning arrow that sailed over the top of Thirsty's head and plunged into the earth near the base of the grandstand. The crowd gasped. All the while, Dan kept talking. Kept selling the story. And it was all I could do to keep my seat, knowing how close I was to meeting Frank again.

"He's bigger than you described him," said Aubrey.

"He's bigger than I remember him. Perhaps he's grown."

My heart raced, and I struggled to control my breathing. I'd quested to find my husband for so long, it seemed impossible that he was standing before me, bathed in sunshine, and looking not a day older than the last time I'd seen him. His humanity had returned; that much seemed evident. This was a man in control of his actions. This was not a mindless killer. I considered on that, and what it might mean for my plans.

"Don't become agitated. This business will soon be concluded," said Aubrey.

"I'm not agitated," I said. "Just impatient."

"As long as we're killing folks," said Aubrey, "I believe old Cowboy Dan would be deserving of the honor too."

Seth grimaced. "Hush that talk. You're just in a sour mood again."

"The man is tiresome."

"Don't mean he needs killing."

"I won't kill him, Seth. I'm just jawing."

"Good, because he puts on a good show."

Thirsty Picket stopped the stage right behind Cowboy Dan. Frank climbed into the shotgun seat, found a rifle there, and aimed it menacingly at the Indians on horseback. Another arrow went flying over the stage and landed right next to the first one. The crowd hissed. Thirsty whooped, urged the team of horses into motion. Cowboy Dan never stopped talking, just raised his voice to be heard over the din as the stagecoach began to circle the arena, slowly gaining speed with each pass. Dan explained that we were about to experience a perfect recreation of his monumental battle with Pawnee raiders, and that the Unkillable Frank Lightning would not only play the part of Cowboy Dan in this drama, but would leave the awestruck crowd with no doubt as to the authenticity of his *unkillable* claim.

Finally, Dan withdrew, and the Indians gave chase.

The *Golden Gulch* continued to circle, now trailed by the Indian riders. Horse hooves rolled like thunder every time they passed the grandstand.

Frank leaned around the side of the stage, fired a few shots over the riders' heads.

The Indians answered with a flurry of arrows. They whispered through the air, struck the back of the stagecoach with a series of dull thuds.

The crowd cheered louder. Blood pounded hard in my head, began to drown out everything else. The performers continued to trade fire, and I wondered at how clinical the whole thing felt. A sanitized version of the violence that had plagued the prairie ever since the European settlers decided to press their way West. This was a performance for romantics, who read about such struggles in dime novels and eastern newspapers. They clapped and laughed and traded jabs with one another about how many Indians they'd have killed if just given the chance and a well-oiled long rifle. My stomach boiled and my heart hurt. None of these people had felt someone's hot blood staining their fine clothes. None of them had smelled death up close. They cheered as the occasional Indian tumbled from his horse, felled by Frank's imaginary bullets, but there was no question the victims would all get back up again. Limbs still attached. Chest cavities untroubled by flattened chunks of lead.

It was a celebration of death, and I hated it.

This all went on for an interminable amount of time, then a rider with a lance pretended to stab Thirsty Picket, and the old man rolled from his seat to the ground. He lay face down pretending to be dead as all those horses raced around him. Given his age, I half expected that sort of tumble to kill him for real. But once the stagecoach and its pursuers were all past, he looked up and gave the crowd a reassuring wink.

Applause erupted.

Frank took the reins, steered the stagecoach with one hand and fired back at the Indians with a pistol.

The brass band started up again; they played at a furious pace.

A rider with a red hand painted on his face came right up alongside the stage, fired an arrow at close range. The flint tip struck Frank square in the stomach. Sunk in deep. Left the shaft and the fletching sticking out of him like a pen from an inkwell.

The crowd gasped. A few people screamed.

There was a great deal of blood.

The band reached a crescendo, and Frank took that as his queue to abandon the stagecoach. The well-trained horses drew the stage to the edge of the arena, clearing the way for the finale.

The Unkillable Frank Lightning.

Alone and surrounded.

The half-dozen riders who hadn't yet fallen to their imaginary deaths took aim and unleashed their arrows in one orchestrated barrage. Every shaft found a home in Frank's body. One in his lower back, a second in his shoulder. Two in his chest and one in his gut. The last one, deep in his right hip. Frank screamed when the arrows struck him, stumbled for a moment like he'd over-indulged on nickel whiskey, then righted the ship and started firing his pistol. He turned in a lazy circle while he did, leaking blood and stumbling, like he was partaking in a difficult dance but hadn't bothered to practice the steps. Indians toppled from horseback. The crowd shrieked and screamed. Bile rose into my throat, and I feared I might vomit. I could feel the world tightening up around me, and the magick going to work once again on Frank's remains. He was full of arrows, but already beginning to heal. When every Indian was dead on the ground, Frank stood heaving for breath, clouded in gun smoke, empty pistol pointed at the sky.

The crown cheered in astonishment.

I wished I was anywhere else in the world.

The dead Indians broke character, stood and waved at the crowd. Thirsty Picket rose from the dead and started pulling the arrows out of Frank. Cowboy Dan joined them, yanking and pulling while Frank grimaced and bled. Nothing had ever horrified me more, apart from my time spent doing the same thing to this man I once loved, so very long ago. Tears streaked my face as the crowd offered a standing ovation. They were sure it was a trick of some sort, and were mightily impressed. Seth rose with them, clapping and hooting, but Aubrey stayed seated next to me, hand still holding mine, his smile banished.

"Allow me to apologize," he said.

"It's okay."

"It appears your Frank might be harder to kill than I imagined."

"He's not my Frank. Not anymore."

"We can go home now," he said. "You can set a new course."

"I really cannot."

"Then I guess we have to see this thing through."

"Was that the finale?"

"It appears so," he said. "It would be hard to top, in any event."

"Then let's go," I said. "This errand can be delayed no longer."

We joined the departing crowd as they filed out of the grandstands, all of them electric with the excitement of what they'd witnessed. Their energy ran through me like so many unloosed arrows, and their joy at the utter *wrongness* of Frank's survival was nearly too much for me to endure. I leaned on Aubrey as we walked. I was unsure on my feet and questioning my choices. But that white specter was everywhere. Peeking out from every eye. Mimicking every high shriek of laughter. I swear I could feel its cold hands on the back of my neck. There really was no choice for me, so I endured the riot of emotion emanating off the crowd. My shoulders shook and my head ached. My breathing came in short bursts. The world was so loud, I felt it driving me to my knees.

I hated my younger self for opening me up to so much pain.

Aubrey found a stand where they were selling food and drinks. He bought me a glass of water, helped me find a place to sit until the crowd diminished.

Hints of nighttime began to creep in and chase away the afternoon. We remained close to the fairground, trying to look inconspicuous, until we judged the camp busy enough that we might move through it without being questioned.

I regained a bit of myself, and we sought out Frank.

Whatever confidence I'd summoned regarding the success of our undertaking had fled. What remained was the sheer terror of being in the same room with Frank again, and a great many questions about how the monster I'd created in Montana could now be trained to perform in a Wild West show, to work the crowd for applause.

None of it made any sense. But the forward trail had been blazed, and I knew nothing else but to follow it.

Seth snooped about and found Frank's tent with little trouble. Seth was in an excitable mood, torn between his enjoyment of the performance, and his growing understanding that there indeed seemed something supernatural about the man he'd come to kill. He led Aubrey and me through the camp, chattering about how big Frank was and asking if we'd seen the way he'd let Thirsty wiggle all those arrows loose without a single squeak. As if we could have missed the spectacle. He questioned whether any of us were in our right minds for carrying on with our mission, and I explained that we most certainly were not. But there was no backing out. By then, we stood in front of the closed tent flap, with gray thunderclouds creeping in overhead again. I called out for admittance before I had another second to talk myself out of it.

"Hello, in the tent!" I said.

I made to knock, but of course there was no door to knock against.

"Come on in."

I wasn't sure whose voice had answered, but I pulled back the tent flap, and we stepped inside.

The Dawson brothers had hands on their holsters.

The interior of the tent was large enough to house a low pine bed covered with disheveled blankets, a wooden chest spilling over with books and clothes, and a folding table where four people had assembled to play dominoes. They sat in wrought iron chairs, and the sound of the dominoes clattering together as one of them shuffled reminded me of Louisa, and the way she was fond of tossing runes to divine her path through the world. I wished intently that she was there to help me, and at the same time wished I'd never met her. A pair of oil lanterns hung from wooden support posts, casting off shadows and coloring everything yellow. Cigarette smoke troubled the upper reaches of the tent space, and everyone seated at the table looked at us like our arrival was not at all unexpected or unwelcomed.

"You have arrived."

"Frank?" I don't know why I posed his name as a question. I knew precisely whom I was addressing. It just seemed impossible we were together again.

"Hello, Catherine," he said. "I've been keeping an eye out for you."

Frank wore nothing but long john underwear, and the visible wounds from his earlier performance still leaked blood. Old scars covered him, and my mind traced each one back to my hands, my surgical skills. My fingertips and my lips and my prayers. He had not aged a day in twenty-six years. Up close I could see the memories of my stitching on his hairless head, and the mottled gray patches that marred his pale green skin. Frank seemed taller than I recalled; even seated he towered over his companions. Like maybe the ritual that brought him back to life had never ended, but instead continued to build and build until he became an impenetrable tower.

"I'm surprised you recognize me," I said.

"How could I not? I see you all the time."

I considered the rituals I used to track Frank down, to watch him from the astral plane as he moved through his days. Was he aware I'd been watching? Was he watching me back? There was too much I needed to know, and I was simply baffled by the fact that Frank appeared in full control of his actions. Last time I'd seen him, Frank had been possessed by something else entirely, and I could not understand how he'd regained himself.

He was smiling, and I noticed his eyes were the same shade of green as when he was alive.

Something turned over inside me, made me light-headed.

Aubrey and Seth stood on either side of me like stone sentinels, obviously as vexed as I was about Frank's casual acceptance of our arrival.

I recognized the people playing dominoes with Frank as performers from the show. The cowboy, Thirsty Picket, the trick shooter Mabel Bones, and the teenaged sharpshooter that Cowboy Dan had called the Hurricane Kid. Thirsty chewed on a pencil, marked down the scoring on a scrap of paper. Mabel offered a polite smile, then went back to studying her dominoes. They could not have been less concerned with the arrival of two armed men. The Kid, however, was all business. He sat straight as a fence post in his chair, hands on his knees like he was posing for a photograph. He watched us with narrowed eyes, and though his hands weren't anywhere close to his holsters, I'd seen how fast he could reach them. I figured he'd make short work of the Dawson brothers, if either were foolish enough to draw down on him.

"You need not stand there and menace us," said Frank. "I'm out of chairs, but you can have a seat on the bed."

"Just move slow," said the Kid.

"I believe we'll stand," I said.

"Who are your companions?" asked Frank.

"Aubrey and Seth Dawson," I said. "Brothers."

"So, you're Frank, then," said Seth.

"That's me."

"Never seen a fellow die and come back to life," said Seth. "That's a hell of a trick, and I will admit to some astonishment. But you don't seem so frightful a character as your wife claims. Appears to me she's exaggerated the reach of your violence, just a mite. You don't look like much of a killer."

"Oh, I'm a killer," said Frank. "Don't doubt it. And if you've come to kill me, make me pay for my past, well, I certainly deserve it."

The tent was stuffy, and Aubrey stood so close I could feel the heat radiating off him. He was smiling again, but I couldn't read what he was thinking. He had a whole collection of smiles. This one might proffer amusement, or it might be a killing grin. The Hurricane Kid had an eager look in his eye, and I hoped Aubrey was paying attention.

"I appreciate you giving us your blessing." Seth's ridiculous top hat still clung to his head, casting him as the fool, but there was no mistaking his readiness for the moment.

"You're not killing anyone," said the Kid.

"Who are you?" Seth's fingers drummed against his pistol grip.

"My name is Hank Abernathy."

"Frank and Hank?" said Seth. "That seems unlikely."

"Ain't neither one of us named ourselves," said Hank. "Just confusing is all."

"Perhaps for the weak minded." Thirsty didn't look up as he spoke, just rearranged the dominoes in front of him, like he was figuring out his next move.

"Joking around can get you shot, old man," said Seth.

"Oh, I don't think he was joking." Mabel Bones spoke in a

pleasant voice, like she was inviting a preacher over for Sunday dinner. But there was mischief in her eyes. Up close, she was beautiful, but younger than I'd realized. Just a few years older than Hank Abernathy, the Hurricane Kid. The barrel of Mabel's long rifle rested against the edge of the table, and there was no question in my mind she could call it to hand in a hurry, if the situation escalated.

"Might want to quiet that girl, cowboy," said Seth.

"Listen to you talk," said Thirsty. "Barking at some old geezer and a girl barely out of pigtails. You're a hard man for sure, ain't you?"

"Hard enough to kill you both where you sit."

Thunder cracked, and wind buffeted the tent.

And in the space of a heartbeat, Hank had a revolver in each hand. One aimed at Seth, the other at Aubrey.

"Well, this is an unnecessary provocation," said Seth.

"Don't pull your pistol," said Hank. "Else we'll have a mess to clean up."

"Aubrey, have you anything to offer?" asked Seth.

"I'd listen to the kid," said Aubrey.

"Perhaps we should withdraw," I said.

Hank shook his head. "Perhaps you should all stay right the hell where you are."

"We've not come to harm anyone," I said.

"I believe you have," said Frank.

"Frank . . ."

"It's alright," he said. "I knew you'd be along to kill me. I'm ready."

"You ain't ready," said Hank.

"Hank, please holster those pistols," said Frank. "You know as well as I do, them coming to kill me doesn't mean a thing at all. Let him shoot me if that's what he wants."

Seth's hand rested heavy on his pistol grip. "Yeah, Hank. Let me shoot him."

"You'll shoot no one," I said.

I was shocked at my sudden reluctance to act. Before me sat the creature I'd hunted for years. Arms wide to welcome his own death. A ravening, bloody killer. Here sat my greatest mistake. Finding a way to kill Frank would not make up for what I'd done, but it would balance the scales of the universe. It would, perhaps, satiate death, and unbind me from my constant hauntings. I'd planned and plotted and dreamed of this moment for so long, and I was certain I'd accounted for every possible outcome in my mental ledger. But not this one. Not my simple refusal to act. I'd expected to come here and find a monster. My astral travels to seek out Frank had shown me enough to know that he'd reclaimed a measure of his humanity. He could walk in the human world without defiling every inch of it. At least in the fleeting moments I followed him. Frank was not ushered out to every show in heavy chains, raging like a wild bull and spitting blood. He was not snapping bones and butchering babies.

Yet I'd been convinced he was still a monster. *He had to be.* Some memories of our time together might have diminished in their intensity, but those last hours at Fort Ellis remained vivid and horrifying in my mind.

Thunder sounded again. I envisioned the lightning storms that passed over the night I brought Frank back from the dead. Such storms, it seemed, were always there to echo our travails, and I could not help but wonder if the very elements of the earth were dark conspirators in our painful drama. At the very least, the hard weather seemed to predict our violence and our grief. Perhaps thunderstorms knew more about the course of our lives than we did.

"You're paying me to kill him," said Seth. "Are you not?"

"I'm no longer certain," I said.

"This is a poor time to go back on a deal," said Seth.

"You'll be paid either way," I said.

"I wouldn't mind you killing me," said Frank.

"See there," said Seth. "He's happy to oblige."

"It's not possible though," said Frank. "I've tried almost everything. You've seen that bullets and arrows are of no use. Poison just gives me a stomachache. Tried to hang myself one time, and I just swung there feeling stupid until somebody cut me down."

"What if I say your act is just a trick?" asked Seth.

"If you shoot me, you'll soon learn it's not."

"Give it a go." Hank was grinning now, still holding his pistols trained on the Dawson brothers. The whole thing appeared to be a game to the Kid, and that made me more nervous than anything. "Frank here likes bullets. They tickle. Thing is, though, you shoot him, you'll catch a bullet next. Might do more than tickle."

"Put away your guns," said Frank. "Anyone wants to shoot me, I'll gladly walk out behind the tent, and you can take aim. Until then, can we just talk?"

Hank slipped his pistols back into their holsters with a sullen look, like shooting someone had been his fondest wish. Seth followed suit. Straightened his top hat and sat down on the bed.

"Have you any whiskey, then?" asked Seth. "If we ain't killing, at least we can start drinking."

"Sorry, no spirits," said Frank. "I don't drink."

"A reservation not shared by your lovely wife." Seth laughed, and Frank looked at me, like he was trying to understand the joke.

The situation was escaping my control. The sight of my hired killer, seated on the sagging mattress, making jokes at my expense to my dead husband was too surreal for me to contemplate long. Seth's words served as reminder to the emptiness inside me, and I tried to remember how long it was since I'd had a drink.

"What about fire?"

Aubrey was still close, and his voice startled me.

"Say what, now?" said Frank.

"Fire," said Aubrey. "Have you tried to burn yourself to death?"

"No, I have not."

"And why is that? Sounds like you're keen on dying."

"The prospect frightens me."

"Worst thing happens, you die."

"No," said Frank. "Worst thing happens is my spirit keeps on living inside a burned-up husk. It's the same reason I haven't asked anyone to cut off my head. What if my spirit remains inside that head? And it keeps on healing, never able to rot away. What kind of life is that? I've lived this way a very long time, and I have it from a reliable source that it was Catherine who cast the spell that left me in this state. She bound my spirit to what's left of this body. But I have no idea how tight a grip her magick has on me, or what would happen if I ruined myself. Worse than that, I don't think she knows either."

Frank's condemnation hit me like slap.

He was bitter about what I'd done to him. Terrified that I'd bound him to eternal life on a sinking ship. And he was right to feel that way.

Seth turned a sour look my way, as if Frank's words confirmed every dark suspicion he fostered about my character. I needed to escape. Needed to go somewhere dark and cold where I could drink and think and regroup. I took a step backward, bumped into Aubrey.

"And if Catherine here can reverse what's she's done?" said Aubrey. "Pluck that soul back out of your body like pulling a weed from the garden. What then?"

"It's not so simple," I said.

My plan all along, were we unable to kill Frank, had been to attempt a ritual to remove his spirit. But in my imaginings, I was taking the soul of a monster. Not a man with a life and friends. Even if he wanted to die, it suddenly felt like murder.

Thirsty Picket glanced up from his dominoes. "All this dying and coming back business makes my head hurt. I figure once I'm dead, I'm liable to stay that way."

"Just say the word, cowboy," said Seth.

The two men had rubbed one another the wrong way out of the gate, and their ire for one another clouded the proceedings.

Thirsty grinned, showed a mouth half full of teeth. He spun the double five domino between his fingers. "I've had bigger boys than you come at me and get turned away in a hurry. You'd do better to talk less and listen more."

"Don't start nothing you can't stop," said Seth.

"Ain't me that started it," said Thirsty. "But keep squealing, little piggie, I'll damn sure be the one to finish it."

"Seth, can you just cool down?" said Aubrey. "Your behavior isn't helping matters."

"My behavior?" said Seth. "We came here to do some killing and now we're supposed to make friends?"

"Everyone wants the same thing," said Aubrey. "There's an easier route to completing our task than expected."

Aubrey was wrong. Not everyone wanted the same thing. I wasn't sure I did anymore. And every time someone talked about killing Frank or taking back his soul, the Hurricane Kid clutched at his pistols.

"Well, I'm not planning to linger while you all dicker about things," said Seth. "I could use a drink."

"I could use one too," said Hank.

Seth laughed again. "You ain't big enough to reach the top of the shot glass."

"Guess I'll just drink yours, once you're dead."

"How old are you, boy?" asked Seth. "Nine or ten? I can't fathom how you've lived this long with a mouth like that."

"I'm fourteen," said Hank. "I recognize that you're an old man, so I won't hold it against you if you can't remember what it was like to be that young."

"We need to leave," I said.

Frank stood for the first time. Lord, he'd become massive.

"Hang on," he said. "Can you really undo this spell?"

I hated the desperate sound of his voice. Hated the way he looked at me like I owed him my soul.

"I don't know that I can," I said.

"But you can try?"

I grabbed Aubrey's arm, pulled him toward the tent flap. "Aubrey, take me back to the hotel. I can't be here any longer. I need to think."

Aubrey seemed put out by the prospect of leaving when we'd come so close to a resolution, but he didn't argue. He nodded at Seth, motioned for him to follow.

Seth groaned theatrically as he stood. "Okay, then. I guess we're going. Gonna stretch out these old bones. Thank you all kindly for the hospitality."

As Seth turned to head our way, he drew his pistol with a speed I hadn't accounted for. He put the barrel against the back of Hank's head.

To his credit, the boy didn't flinch.

"You ain't the only one who's fast and fancy," said Seth.

"I'll write that down, so it don't slip my mind," said Hank.

Seth spun his pistol with a flourish, and deposited it back into his holster.

"Don't forget, kid, I could have killed you."

"Keep on thinking that," said Hank.

"Seth! Let's go." Aubrey grabbed his brother by the arm, pulled him from the tent.

I was already hurrying through the camp, desperate to escape. Rain pounded the earth, and death hounded my heels. Lightning flashed just beyond the edge of the fairgrounds, and I prayed the next bolt would strike me dead, so I didn't have to face all the pain that was sure to follow.

Draw Down the Lightning
The Bloody Frontier, Montana Territory
Autumn 1879

THE VALLEY WAS A KILLING FIELD.

Eleven bodies, torn and scattered. Cavalry uniforms stiff with dried blood. The land was furrowed and blackened by cannon balls, and the air smelled of cinders and rot. I climbed down from the wagon as soon as Falling Bird slowed, and I dove into the carnage, in search of Frank. Some of the men were intact, faces looking skyward. They might have been sleeping if not for the arrows protruding from their chests. Others had encountered cannon fire, and those bodies were ruined beyond recognition. Every man had been scalped; bloody skulls glistened in the fading daylight. Carrion birds picked at the dead, flitting away with a shriek when I moved past, then settling back to their meals.

My frantic search eventually turned up Frank's body. There was no doubt he'd met his end from a ball filled with powder. The explosion had taken his right arm at the shoulder, and shredded his chest. Both of his legs were missing below the knee, one cauterized black and the other with a jagged length of bone protruding. A couple of arrows angled out from one hip, and there was a bullet hole in his throat. Like the others, his scalp had been roughly cut away. The birds or other scavengers had chewed through his uniform. I knelt beside him, gently lifted his eyelids, and was grateful to see they hadn't taken his eyes.

I fell atop him. Took his cold corpse into my arms.

Dark clouds marched down from the mountains, and heavy winds rushed through the valley. The grass swayed and I swear I could hear the dead whispering through the tall blades. Falling Bird stood beside me, rifle in hand, eyes studying the horizon. We were more than a day's ride from the fort, and he was worried the attackers would return; I did not share his concern. I was ready to die there on the ground.

Falling Bird had not exaggerated Frank's condition. My confidence now seemed misplaced. So much of him was simply *gone*. How could I summon what remained of his soul back into this broken shell? I wept for a time. Wallowed in defeat and uncertainty as I pressed my ear against his ruined chest and listened for his missing heartbeat. What were my options? To leave his body to rot in that valley, a meal for every hungry animal, or to carry his broken corpse back to Fort Ellis, where it could be buried in that lonely churchyard, fretted over by young Preacher Meek.

Neither of these outcomes would satisfy my desires.

Louisa always told me that magick was about a person wielding their *will*. Reshaping reality to match the image of what they wished it to be. She'd been so adamant about this simple truth. Every ritual, every prayer, every long hour spent meditating on ancient symbols and seeking out links to other realities, were all in service to that truth. It was the core of what the Three Rose Temple and other similar esoteric orders believed. And yet, when my will had been to deliver my parents back from the dead, Louisa had recoiled at the notion. The Three Rose Temple had admonished me for leaving the true path. Cautioned me about *low magick* and consorting with the wrong sorts of spirits. For all their talk about mastering our own realities, when it came to the ultimate questions about life and death, their teachings were academic. Fearful, even. And when Louisa flatly refused to help me bring my parents back, when she delayed my efforts too long for me to even have the chance, our life together was over, and my tutelage with the Three Rose Temple was finished.

But I'd never stopped studying. Never stopped forming new rituals of my own.

The Three Rose Temple had ultimately failed me.

I would not, in turn, fail my husband.

As I lay atop him, I slowed my breathing, allowed myself to fall into a sort of surface-level meditation. Not a trance state, not a deep dive into the ethereal realm, but close enough that I could listen to the spirits in that wild place. Close enough to seek their assistance and find if anything remained of Frank. They were all so lonely. They rushed in close, eager to make themselves known before I cut the connection. There were souls of people long dead, burdened with eternity, yet unable to progress to their next lives. And there were spirits with no ties to humanity, that had existed in that low valley for eons. Creatures of wind and rock and cleansing fire. Beings gilded with starlight and aswarm with shadows. Unknowable things that chased through my mind like rampaging nightmares, and more pleasant entities that felt like rivers of cool water flowing over me.

Somewhere in that chaos was Frank.

I whispered prayers, promised offerings. Begged and pleaded for one of those spirits to help me find my husband.

And after a long time, I found him.

He was not aware of my presence, but his being was unmistakable. His soul, his energy, his *essence*, had not yet moved on.

I wasn't too late.

My eyes snapped open, and I sat up, gasping in the cold air. Long shadows drew paths across the valley, and the sun would soon be gone.

"Can you please erect the tent?" I asked.

Falling Bird looked at once sympathetic and baffled. When I made to stand on unsteady legs, he helped me to my feet. "The tent is for emergencies. We can't stay here tonight."

"The work I need to do, I don't want to do it outside," I said. "I'm afraid it might storm again."

"We have to ride for the fort," said Falling Bird. "As soon as we load Frank into the wagon."

"His spirit is here. It won't find his body anywhere else. We aren't riding for the fort tonight."

"Catherine, we are not safe here."

"There's no safe place for what has to be done."

"I understand your desperation, but I don't want to die for it."

"If you want to ride back at once, I won't fault you. Please leave me the tent and the supplies, and I can manage the rest on my own."

"I'm not going to leave you . . ."

"Then you have little choice but to help me, so we can be on our way as soon as possible," I said. "Please hurry with the tent while I make other preparations."

Once again, I felt guilty for placing Falling Bird in such a dangerous situation, when there was no certainty my ritual would bear fruit. But there was no time for soft manners or coaxing words. No room for reservations. If everything worked to plan, we'd escape this valley soon enough, and carry Frank home with us, alive.

Falling Bird unloaded the tent poles and the brown roll of canvas, began to assemble the shelter. He labored in silence, no longer choosing to argue with a person he surely considered insane. I made another quick inspection of Frank's body, and girded myself for the terrible task before me. Frank's missing appendages would have to be replaced. From the cluttered insides of my large leather bag, I withdrew Dr. Prosper's bone saw. I then walked among the dead, seeking out suitable parts to replace those Frank had lost. I cannot imagine what Falling Bird must have thought as I patrolled the battlefield with a saw in hand, taking stock of the dead. But he'd had his fill of me, and continued working without comment. I fear his sympathy had leaked away, leaving only bitter resolve. When I finally located a young man not dissimilar in size to my husband, his body largely intact, I knelt beside him, whispered a prayer for his soul, and went about the grisly job of removing his limbs.

It was not delicate work.

I'd used a saw on the living before, but never on the dead. There seemed little to differentiate one from another, save the lack of screaming. The man's mortified flesh was already green with decay in some areas, and when the saw teeth caught the bone, it jerked in my hand, made a terrible raspy sound, and I had to bear down to keep the blade moving. There is no doubt I was half out of my mind with desperation in that moment, but I carried on, reassuring myself that the ritual would make allowances for imperfect bodies. So the text had claimed, and I'd read every word I'd copied down over and over in the years since my parents died, absorbing it into my bones, in the event I might have cause to perform it. The magick inherent in the ritual would heal even massive wounds. It would seal torn flesh and repair ruptured organs. Broken bones would mend, and blood and breath would flow again. So long as Frank's body was substantially intact, the magick would do the rest. I had no assurances, however, that it would regrow lost limbs, so I continued to saw. My muscles began to ache from the effort, and sweat burned my eyes, but eventually the deed was done.

By the time I finished, the tent was standing. Falling Bird staked it to the ground, but the howling wind tore at the canvas sides, giving the impression the tent might soon take flight. Whatever reprieve we'd had from the weather came to an end, and the rain fell in a fury.

"Help me move him," I said.

Falling Bird helped me drag Frank's body inside the tent, his face a grim mask of disbelief and horror. I hurried outside, gathered the arms and legs I'd collected, brought them all inside and tied the tent flaps closed.

"This is a wicked thing you do," said Falling Bird.

"Your protestations have become tiresome." I wiped away the rain and the sweat from my brow with a dry towel from my bag, removed a long needle and catgut thread. Falling Bird had unloaded a lantern, and I lit it, hung it from a canvas loop at the top of the tent.

"Frank wouldn't want this."

"We disagree on the matter, and I've given you leave to depart. Must you continue to harass me?"

Falling Bird withdrew to the corner of the tent, sat on the hard ground, back bent with fatigue and disgust. He occupied the shadows in cold silence as I used a scalpel to debride the rotted flesh around Frank's shoulder. Rain sounded like a freight train travelling over the canvas. I cleaned away all the rot and debris from the shoulder, then did the same everywhere else. I dug my hands into Frank's chest and put him back together as best as I could, trusting the magick would do the heaviest share of the work. Then I set about attaching new limbs, threading my silver needle through loose skin, and drawing the thread taut.

I recall being inordinately proud of myself in that moment. For whom but someone with my unique combination of medical training and esoteric learning could have undertaken such a bold and frightful task? The fact that my thoughts traveled to such a prideful place in those dark moments, where even my personal grief became momentarily subservient to my ambitions, stands testament to the fact that I was operating from a place of hubris and not entirely one of love.

I couldn't understand then, what's plain to me now.

The new arms and legs weren't perfect matches, but I worked them onto Frank's body as carefully as I could. They were freckled and pale and almost hairless. I found myself wondering about the man from whom I'd stolen them. How old was he, and where was he from? What would his family think about the way his body was being abused? These thoughts I banished as quickly as they arose, tried to focus only on my work, but they kept returning, like the man's ghost intended to haunt me for the indignity I'd caused. Maybe that was exactly what was happening. Who could blame him? The legs and arm now attached, I hurried out into the rain, returned moments later with a length of ashen skin from the same soldier's back, and properly sized a piece to replace Frank's scalp. Likewise, I used the skin to repair other places where Frank's own had been torn away, or ruined beyond repair. It was anxious, tedious work. It was gruesome and foul. But I managed to rebuild him, make him physically whole.

The magick would have to do the rest.

Falling Bird remained motionless throughout the surgery, cloaked in shadows. The tent was a small A-frame with cedar support poles on either end. He sat near the back pole with one hand holding it firm against the buffeting wind. The rain had not abated, and my labors kept us there deep into the night. Falling

Bird's eyes caught the lantern light, and they did not waver. He studied my progress, like I was a dangerous animal who might come after him next with my scalpel. Like I was a madwoman hungry for violence. When my work was done, I remained seated beside Frank's body, trying to catch my breath. The physical labor of repairing the body was only the beginning. The ritual remained, and it would be so much more taxing. I closed my eyes for a time, listened to the rain. When Falling Bird finally spoke, it was as sudden and unexpected as a voice from the afterlife.

"This is a terrible, terrible thing you've done."

"What have I done?" I asked. "Put him together is all. You think I'm finished? This was the easy bit."

"Now comes the witchcraft?"

"Now comes my husband, back from the dead! Your great friend, back from the dead! Now comes an absolute miracle! And I shall perform it, whether you believe it's possible or not. All I require from you is your distance. Once I begin the ritual, do not think to disrupt it. No matter how incredulous you may be, trying to end things once they've started will result in calamity for both of us."

"I won't meddle with your spell."

Satisfied he would not, I opened my bag and began preparing everything I needed for the ritual. Blood darkened my fingers. The wretched odor of decay suffused the tent; I lit a bit of palo santo wood, but even that would not chase away the awful smell. I let the smoke drift about the room to clear away any beings who might see fit to work against me, then I lit a mixture of frank-incense and myrrh in a censer and gave it some time to help set the spiritual table, so to speak, for what would come next. In the meantime, I opened my book on the ground beside me, read over everything again to make sure I had forgotten nothing. Frank still lay motionless against the earth, and I used a stone to carve a circle into the hard ground, surrounding him completely.

Within the circle, I carved powerful symbols.

In the space between Frank's legs, I carved a circle, within a square, within a triangle, within a larger circle. Something the old alchemists used to symbolize the philosopher's stone, a representation of eternal life. Over his head, I carved the symbol for Mercury, a sigil that would ease his soul in overcoming death. Above him, below him, at his sides, I carved symbols signifying the four elements—air, water, earth, and fire—and I spoke my intentions aloud in an arrhythmic chant. Other symbols emerged as I continued to carve. Older, less familiar shapes. A sort of geometry of the dead that I'd never seen outside of old books and my own hazy dreams. Only my faith and my desperation gave me confidence in their power.

After I'd finished this, I took up my scalpel, and carved the symbol for Mercury into Frank's naked chest.

Falling Bird hissed, but he did not interfere.

Next, I removed myself from the circle and performed a banishing ritual. Another assurance against the meddling of external forces. Nothing outside the perimeter of the tent should be able to enter lest I will it. I lit four candles at the perimeter of the circle, one for each direction. Lit two more and held them in my hands. One flame for above, one for below. Then I called to the four winds, recited the words over and over until the air grew cold and heavy, and the candle flames flickered in the stillness.

I began to chant. Reading aloud from my black book at first, repeating the same verses time after time, until eventually the words came to life in my throat, shouted themselves into existence with no help from me. I abandoned the book, and the chant continued. This was a call to Hermes, god of the way, lord of liminality, begging his aid and that of his servants, to bring Frank's soul into this place, into this circle, into this *body*. Hermes served many roles in the magickal traditions taught by the Three Rose Temple, but in that moment, I envisioned him in his capacity as a psychopomp, a being who escorts souls between the land of the living, and the land of the dead. Hermes trod the paths of the underworld with regularity and ease. And if Hermes could guide souls toward their next existence, it stood to reason he could lead them back to their old lives too.

The storm intensified. Wind shook the tent and rain fell in a violent torrent, causing the canvas to sag around us. Lightning broke brightly, and loud thunder followed with unsettling speed.

It was like the storm had been waiting for this, like it had anticipated the ritual.

I did not know it then, but that storm would follow me for the rest of my life.

A charge sizzled through the room, caused the hair on my arms to lift and sway. That energy fed the ritual, clarified my thoughts, and I could envision Hermes himself, standing in winged sandals on a road lined with rough stones, souls flowing past him like fish in the sea. Snakes coiled around his rough-hewed staff, and he watched the souls move up and down that road with a serene smile. A black river churned behind him, spanned by a crude wooden bridge. Weary cypress trees lined the shore, their branches populated with owl eyes that glimmered and blinked and studied the passage of souls with dark curiosity. I understood instinctively what lay beyond the river. The land of the dead. The true afterlife. Should Frank cross over that bridge, even Hermes would not consent to return him to me.

My voice became a scream. The words burned my throat.

Hermes turned his head, saw me, and smiled.

Turning back was out of the question now.

The air grew so heavy around me that I could feel it compressing my chest, making it harder to breathe, harder to chant. The storm sounded like a mountain collapsing around us. Falling Bird began screaming something, but I could not hear him. Part of me watched Frank's body begin to buck like it was being touched with an electrical charge, and the rest of me studied Hermes as he searched for Frank's soul in the sudden rush of beings who became drawn in by the ritual. There were thousands of them. More. Those who remembered life and were desperate to return. Those who had never lived at all, but sought an escape from this unreal place. Shadows swarmed and souls shone like miniature suns. Tears fell down my cheeks, and my voice became a whisper as the atmosphere continued to constrict. When I could no longer breathe, I continued the ritual words in my mind, desperately hoping that Hermes could still hear me. That he'd grant me this boon before I passed out from lack of oxygen, and the ritual fell apart.

Hermes reached out, snatched Frank's brightly glowing soul from the center of the chaos.

He smiled, and offered it to me.

There existed no equal to the storm that raged outside our tent.

Thunder boomed like artillery fire.

Falling Bird backed up to the far edge of the space, wanting distance from Frank's shuddering body, but unwilling to brave the deadly barrage of lightning. Thunder rolled, one explosion on top of the other, until it became a single resonant voice, taunting us in a language humans could not understand. Blood coursed from my nose, from my ears, and Falling Bird was still yelling something, but I'd found my voice again, and I howled back at the storm. I screamed my demands to the universe.

I *willed* Frank's soul back into his body.

After that, unreality took hold. It's hard to recall exactly what happened, but I remember it like this:

A lightning bolt tore through the canvas, struck Frank squarely in the chest. White light consumed the world, and the force of the blast threw me from the tent. Darkness claimed me for a time, and when I woke, the canvas was shredded, the tent poles snapped, and the storm had passed. Every corpse in the valley was blackened by lightning. Our team of horses was in a similar state, and our wagon had been reduced to kindling. My dress was covered in blood, and my throat felt like I'd swallowed glass shards. There was a moment of disorientation as I sat on the ground, wondering where I was and how I'd gotten there. Then I saw Frank lying on his back, and Falling Bird kneeling beside him. I crawled over to where they were, everything coming back to me in a rush.

Falling Bird had one hand on Frank's forehead, the other on his chest. When I got close, Falling Bird grabbed my wrist, put my hand where his had been against Frank's chest. There was a heartbeat. There was movement in his lungs. The body was warm. Was not, in fact, a *body* any longer. Falling Bird watched for my reaction, stared at me with a mixture of terror and elation. When I did not react, he gave my shoulder a gentle shake, like he meant to rouse me from a light slumber. No matter how hopeful I'd been about the ritual, I'd never been certain. There was a large part of me that believed I was chasing madness, and perhaps that's what happened. Perhaps I was kneeling beside a dead body, willing myself to believe it had returned from the dead. Fooling myself into thinking I had found the one soul I sought and stolen it back from the shores of the river of the dead.

It was an impossibility, but that didn't make it any less real.

"Catherine? Are you okay?"

That was not a question I was ready to answer.

"Do you understand what's happened?" he asked. "Frank's moving. He's moving!"

"Yes."

"He's alive!" A grin broke across Falling Bird's face.

"What?"

"Alive! He's alive!"

The weight of what I'd done fell upon me. I lay down across my husband, there in the cold and muddy place of his death, and I let my exhaustion claim me.

The Storm Survivor
The Silver Ace, Fort Worth, Texas
Spring 1905

THE DAWSON BROTHERS had tolerated my eccentricity throughout our travels together, but both men were baffled at my reluctance to undertake the task that had brought us to Texas. Seth had demonstrated his taste for killing, and was irritated that his hunger had so far gone unsatisfied. Aubrey had a more pragmatic take on things. My expressed desire to kill Frank, or otherwise remove his soul with a ritual, had been met with little resistance. Even the target of our intended violence was an eager and willing accomplice to the deed. In Aubrey's eyes, we'd been presented a simple resolution to our business. A transaction, however bleak, that all found amenable.

But they could not understand what had changed for me in that tent. Frank was a different person now; that was certain. But he still sounded the same. I could hear that voice speaking promises about our future together. And the life had returned to his eyes. Last time I saw them, they'd been bright with violence and void of emotion. Now he could *see me* again. All the trauma he'd undergone was there, but so was the longing, and maybe even the memory of love.

Despite *everything.*

My choice would have been so much easier if he'd simply remained a monster.

I could never kill him now. Not even to save myself.

As if to acknowledge my reluctance, my spectral tormentor unfolded from the dark corners of the Silver Ace and drifted across the floor like a thin layer of white fog. I closed my eyes. Wished for it to leave me alone. I gripped a bottle of whiskey. I'd been back at the Silver Ace for an hour, and it was already half empty. The Dawson brothers seemed to have had their fill of me. Seth stayed long enough for a shot of rye, then ventured out into the night, in search of trouble. Aubrey tried to figure out my plans, but eventually he left me alone too. I assured the brothers they'd receive the balance of their payment when the banks opened in the morning, and whatever course of action I decided on, I would undertake without their assistance. Aubrey took that hard. He'd become overfond of me, I think. And I'd let him. I cannot say my heart didn't share that growing fondness, but I'd learned long ago to keep sentiment at arm's length.

When I opened my eyes, the specter sat in the chair beside me. White, smokey, vaguely human shaped. Testing the air with wispy tentacles. So close I could feel it pulling at my soul.

I lifted the whiskey bottle in mock salute. "Never fear, demon. You'll have me soon enough."

The specter didn't respond.

Business had slowed at the Silver Ace, but there were still a few cowboys lined up at the bar. Their talk and their laughter and their clinking glasses sounded a thousand miles away, as if the specter and I existed in our own separate world. Rain continued to pour outside, and wind caused the swinging doors to shudder on their hinges. The room was hot, and so muggy it felt like I was floating underwater. Everything had gone soft around the edges, either a product of my rapid ingestion of alcohol, or a trick the specter was playing on my brain. Either way, it didn't matter. I was ready to relent.

The specter seemed to understand; smoke billowed out from its chest, circled my chair in an embrace. Pulled me closer to the table.

I took a deep breath.

Imagined taking all that smoke into my lungs and just *letting go*.

"Ma'am, are you okay?"

I looked up to see Hank Abernathy, the Hurricane Kid, standing across the table. He couldn't see the specter; nobody else could, as far as I could tell. But the way he looked at me, he might as well have been looking at a corpse. My fine dress was still soaked, and my hair fell long across my face. I felt bloodless and grim, and it must have shown in my expression. Hank slid a chair back, took a seat. He took off his straw hat, placed it on the table in front of the specter. The thing shifted, ever so slightly. Moved closer to Hank. It looked less like smoke now, and more like water streaks on a windowpane.

"Thank you," I said. "I'm fine."

"You appear distressed."

I choked up a laugh. "I cannot imagine what's brought me to such a state."

"Is there something I can do to help?"

"Why are you here, Hank?"

"Well, I just wanted to talk. To meet you. Maybe to apologize for my rude manner back there. I'm usually the friendly sort. Your men, coming in there with guns, it elevated my dander."

"You've no need to apologize," I said. "Just go. We won't trouble you again."

"Frank has talked to me about you."

"Has he? And what's he told you?"

"Nothing bad, I promise."

"I don't believe that for a second."

The notion of Frank remembering anything about me, let alone sharing those memories, was a concept I couldn't quite apprehend. If anything, I must exist in his recollections as the stupid woman who misused her magick and doomed him to a life of ruin. Whatever good memories we'd shared were surely overshadowed by how it all ended.

Hank pulled a cigarette from his shirt pocket, lit it with the oil lamp that sat on the table. He leaned back in his chair, glanced about the room like he was settling in for the evening.

"Is the food here edible?" he asked.

"Hank, I wish you'd leave me alone."

"My stomach's growling."

"Then order a steak and eat it at another table."

"You're not real sociable, are you," said Hank.

"I'm working on getting blind drunk," I said. "I'd prefer it be a solitary undertaking."

Hank kept puffing his cigarette, eyeing me like he was still trying to decipher what sort of person I really was.

"I don't believe he understands what kind of spell you used to bring him back," said Hank.

"Spell? All right."

"Whatever you call it," said Hank. "Whatever you did. But he's sorted out some things along the way. He's learned enough to know you used *supernatural gifts*. That's what he called them, *supernatural gifts*. He said y'all weren't together long, but you put a hook in his heart and reeled him in quick. Those are his words, again. He's told me all about Fort Ellis. The last thing he was thinking, when all them Sioux rode down into that valley, arrows flying? Frank was just sad he'd never see you again. And he never did. Until now, I guess."

"I need you to stop talking, Hank."

"Frank is my friend," said Hank. "Don't have too many of those."

"I'm not going to harm him."

"But you came here thinking you would."

"Circumstances have changed."

Anger blossomed inside me, and I came close to lashing out. Then I took a good look at him and remembered he was just a boy. The way he'd fearlessly engaged with Seth, and the way he handled his pistols made it easy to forget he was not yet fifteen years old. He sat leaned back in his chair, one hand casually on his pistol grip, trying his best to look like the grown man he'd become if he didn't get himself shot first. He chewed on the thumbnail of his other hand, cigarette still gripped in between his fingers, and he kept throwing looks over at the door, like he was afraid someone would hunt him down and send him home to bed. I had no idea how a child could end up making friends with a man like Frank, or plying his shooting skills in *Cowboy Dan's Wild West Revue*. Whatever the circumstances, they were likely unpleasant, and when I spoke again to Hank, I controlled myself and proceeded in a more sympathetic voice.

"Yes, I came here planning to kill him. But I hadn't realized he . . . regained himself? You must understand, Frank was a monster."

"He admits as much."

"Tell him I'm leaving," I said. "Soon as I can. I won't harm him."

"There is the problem. He *wants* you to harm him. He's tired of living, I guess. Or at the very least, tired of *halfway* living. That's something I understand."

"How so?"

Hank shrugged, inhaled a lungful of smoke.

"Smoking's a nasty habit," I said.

Hank eyed my whiskey bottle and laughed. "There's worse habits to have."

"Perhaps, but you're too young for any of them."

"Might be I've grown up faster than most."

"Then let us indulge our vices in silence."

"I won't trouble you long," said Hank. "I only desired some clarity on matters. Like I told you, Frank is my friend. And he wants to die. Might be selfish of me, but I ain't ready to cut him loose yet. He's liable to come here and demand you undo your spell. You must stand strong. You must refuse him. Else, you and me will be at odds. That would be an unpleasant development."

His threat could not have affected me less. If he'd pulled his pistol to shoot me then, I would have risen to my feet, to offer him a bigger target.

"You take all this magickal thinking in stride."

"I'm accustomed to strangeness," he said. "My sister is a witch. She can read your mind, tell the future sometimes. Can you do that sort of thing?"

"No, nothing like that." How could I explain to him that the future had little allure? It was the past that held me in sway.

"But you *are* a witch, ain't you?"

"Not exactly a witch," I said, "but you're not far off the mark."

"I figured," said Hank. "Lot of folks think witches are wicked, but every witch I ever met was a kind soul with a good heart."

"You've met a lot of good-hearted witches, have you?"

"Three, I guess. My sister, my mother, and you."

"Don't be so sure my heart is pure."

"If you didn't have a decent nature," said Hank, "Frank wouldn't think so highly of you."

"Where's your mother and your sister now?" I asked.

"My mother burned up in a house fire. My father too. My sister still lives in Galveston, I reckon. But I ain't going back there to seek confirmation."

"I'm sorry about your parents."

"It was people in our town burned the house down around them. Hated my mother for being a witch."

"They murdered your parents?"

"That's *exactly* what they did."

"Oh, lord . . . that's horrifying."

"It certainly altered my outlook on life."

"What about your sister? Why are you travelling with the Wild West Revue instead of going home to Galveston? Did you have a falling out?"

"No, we were always close. It ain't my sister that repels me, it's the place. You die somewhere, it leaves you disinclined to visit again."

"You don't look dead."

"Well, I am."

"That's not a topic I find funny."

"I'm not making a joke, ma'am."

"You are telling me you're dead?"

"Not anymore," said Hank. "But I used to be."

That caused me to take a long pull off my bottle of whiskey. Long enough that Hank screwed up his face into a scowl, like he was rethinking his notions on how proper women were supposed to behave.

What Hank said was far-fetched, but who was I to scoff at the notion of resurrection?

Perhaps this was a ruse he'd concocted with Frank; perhaps they had designed some elaborate plan for revenge that would only reveal itself once I'd taken the bait.

Either way, it didn't matter.

If Frank wanted to ruin me, I'd gladly let him.

But if Hank was telling the truth, maybe I could learn what went wrong with my ritual. Maybe if I had more clarity on the nature of the afterlife, I could resolve decades of mistakes. Encountering another soul returned from the dead stretched the bounds of probability. But my studies in the supernatural world had left me well acquainted with strange synchronicities.

I finished off my bottle, welcomed the whiskey heat into my chest.

"I suppose you need to explain yourself."

Hank finished his cigarette, stubbed it out underneath his boot. Patted his shirt pocket looking for another, but came up empty.

"I guess you heard about the Galveston hurricane?"

Of course, I had. Everyone had. It was the worst storm to ever hit the Texas coast. Any coast, for all I knew. Storm enough that it made the papers nationwide. A terrible hurricane that erased the island city of Galveston from the map, like someone wiping a rag across a chalkboard. Towering walls of water, and wind that carried away people and wagons and houses. Upwards of ten thousand people died in that storm. And five years later, Galveston was still working hard to rebuild all it had lost.

The Great Storm, they were already calling it.

"I read about it when it happened," I said.

"Well, I drowned in that storm."

Instead of a cigarette, Hank removed an iron nail from his shirt pocket, set it gently on the tabletop. He spun it in circles as he spoke.

"I was a kid then, of course."

Hank was still a kid, but I didn't tell him that.

Hank wasn't looking at me anymore. He kept his eyes on that nail as he fumbled with it.

"When they burned down our house, my sister and me were there. We'd have burned up too, but our mother had enacted a spell. I told you, she was a witch."

"You did."

"I think she knew them people were coming for her. I can't speak on how her magick worked, but she put something of herself into three iron nails. This one here, and two others. And Nellie said . . . Nellie is my sister. She said that's the only reason me and her walked away from that fire unscathed. This wasn't in Galveston. Not yet."

Despite the whiskey clouding my head, and the heat of the room pressing in on all sides like a suffocating blanket, I found myself focused on the boy's every word. My eagerness for answers dissolved into the simple desire to learn more about what had brought him here. Both the magickal paths and the mundane. He spun the nail around and around, and I wondered what sort of power his mother had put into that simple bit of metal that had saved her children's lives.

The specter became stone-still, like it was listening too.

"So, anyways," said Hank, "me and my sister were made orphans."

"I'm sorry."

"There are kind people in this world, ma'am. Some of them took us in."

"There aren't many," I said. "Glad you found some."

"More out there than you think," said Hank.

"So, these generous souls took you to Galveston?"

"Yeah, Floyd took us there. And Charlie, I guess."

Hank never looked up from his nail, but a grin spread across his young face.

"Where'd you meet them?"

"That's not the story I'm telling right now."

"Sorry."

"We encountered more challenges. But we ended up in a boardinghouse a short way from the beach, and that's where we were when the storm hit. Nellie had reclaimed the nails from the embers of our old home, and she hammered them into the wall of the boardinghouse, like they might keep us attached to the beach. I guess she thought some of Mother's power was still inside them. She did not explain her actions at the time, and I was dead not long after that. I haven't seen her since."

"What was it like, being dead?" It was a terrible thing to ask him, but I couldn't help myself.

"I have no memories of that."

"Then how do you know you died?"

"When it happens to you, you'll understand what a stupid question that is."

Rain continued marching overhead, and I wondered if it would ever stop again.

"Whatever happened, the storm carried me a long way off," said Hank. "When I opened my eyes, I was halfway to Houston. And I was holding tight to this nail. How did I even get it? There's no way possible. Except that my mother's spell is still working. That's all I can figure. I think whatever she did to this nail, it brought me back from the dead. Do you think that's what happened?"

Hank finally looked up at me, leaned close over the table. He looked younger than ever. His face was rosy from the heat, his cheeks smooth and hairless. My fear that he might be trying to deceive me vanished. Circumstances had crafted a vulnerability in this boy that would be impossible for him to fake. Every moment of bluster now seemed a defense against the world, by a lost and searching child.

"Maybe that's exactly what happened," I said. "Your mother obviously loved you very much."

Hank nodded, put the nail back in his shirt pocket.

"Your friends, did they all die?"

"I don't know," said Hank.

"But you said your sister is alive. Are you sure?"

"She has a *way* about her," said Hank. "If she was dead, I'd know it."

"Part of her witchy nature?"

"That's right."

"But you won't go to Galveston to see her? Does she even know you survived?"

"I didn't survive."

"You understand my meaning, Hank."

"I left something there," he said. "Some part of myself. Don't know how to explain, but maybe it's part of my soul. Or my ghost? That sounds ridiculous. Can a person be haunted by their own ghost?"

I'd never heard of anything like he described in all my time studying the mysteries. But I didn't doubt it could happen. In my experience, a person could be haunted by pretty much anything.

My head was swimming too much to focus and find Hank's aura, but I remembered how gray and transparent it had appeared during his performance. It was unlike any I'd ever seen, and now I understood why. Hank Abernathy was not entirely *there*. Like Frank, he was an uncanny shadow of the person he'd been. Illuminated by death. A scared young boy carrying the weight of the afterlife around with him. No wonder he felt so close to Frank. They were of a kind. And no matter how many nice things Frank might say about me, how could this boy look at me and see anything but the woman who'd traveled hundreds of miles to kill the only real family he had left in the world?

A woman who'd brought bloody killers with her.

As if on cue, Seth Dawson walked into the Silver Ace.

"Your boon companion returns," said Hank.

"We are hardly friends," I said.

Seth was exceedingly drunk, far beyond my somewhat compromised state. He strode forward on unsteady feet, pausing occasionally to look down at the floor, seeking confirmation that firm ground remained beneath his boots. His coat was missing and one of his shirtsleeves torn, and he'd muddied his pants up one side, giving the impression that he'd fallen somewhere along the way. By some small miracle the top hat remained adhered to his head. When he noticed Hank and me, sitting at the table, he slowed his approach, squinted through the smokey air like we might be twin visions he could blink away. Seth then came to a full stop, checked absently to make sure his holster remained on his hip, and stared us down with glassy eyes.

"Hello, Doc," he said. "Consorting with the enemy now, are you?"

"This boy is not our enemy."

"Might not be yours, but he's sure as hell mine."

"Let me buy you a steak, Seth."

"Thank you, no. I have already eaten."

"Seth, this boy has done nothing more than pull your leg. He's a child."

"A child who requires discipline. Have you a leather strap or a switch handy? I can put the pup over my knee."

The sound of chair legs against the cedar floorboards announced Hank's intentions. He stood, packed all his emotions back into his chest other than his anger. Moments before, Hank had offered me the gift of his vulnerability, but that vanished the instant Seth approached. Hank seemed to grow loose and limber as he rose, and I imagined I could see the recklessness running through his blood and animating his actions. Hank's hands were nowhere near his guns, but violence lurked in the margins.

"The young shootist rises to defend himself." Seth cut loose with a wet laugh, staggered but regained his footing.

Hank summoned his resolve. "Remove yourself from this place, scoundrel."

"What is that you called me?"

"Scoundrel. I've dispatched your like before, and I am confident I can do it again."

The room spun in circles, and I felt the weight of circumstances pulling me to my knees.

"Hank, you should leave," I said. "Quickly please."

"Hank will remain here," said Seth. "We've matters yet to resolve."

"We have nothing left to discuss," said Hank. "Other than your swift departure."

"You'll not move me, boy."

"You'll pass out soon enough, you trifling fool."

"I fear you have misjudged me," said Seth. "For I am a very serious man."

Seth moved with a suddenness that belied his drunken state. Found his pistol grip and drew with a speed born of long practice and misspent years. But his aim was not yet level when shots echoed, and the acrid scent of gunpowder assaulted the air. Seth spun, toppled. Struck the floor face down. No matter how fervently I might wish it was not the case, Seth Dawson was stone-cold dead.

The Hurricane Kid had put four bullets in his chest.

Colt revolvers occupied both of Hank's hands. He held them close to his hips, having fired double shots from both guns immediately upon removal from their holsters. His slim body trembled. Lantern light spilled down both barrels. Two of the other patrons hustled out the swinging doors, and the others took refuge behind the bar. Rain sliced through the darkness beyond the doorway, and lightning splashed against the windows. Seth Dawson remained face down on the hardwood. Blood pooled beneath him; it spread out from both shoulders like he was growing a set of angel wings. So much blood, I could not imagine much remained inside him. Panic suffused the stillness. I could hear the rapid chatter of the men behind the bar, and the gasping sound of Hank's breathing. Seth's death filled the room with a vile odor, and a shudder ran up Hank's spine as he stood over the dead man, taking stock of the carnage he'd wrought.

"I have never . . ." he said. "I had not expected him to draw."

I advanced on Hank, slow and deliberate so as not to spook him. I placed a hand on his shoulder, felt the heat of his fear. "Holster your guns, Hank. If you would."

Hank complied. "We must summon a doctor."

"He is beyond such help," I said.

"*You're* a doctor, ain't you?" said Hank. "If you hurry, you can mend him."

"I cannot. He's dead."

"If he's dead, then I'll hang."

"You fired to defend yourself. There are those here who will surely swear to it. And so will I."

Hank shook his head, shrugged my hand away from his shoulder. His eyes grew red and teary. For all his youthful bluster, there was no mistaking this was the first time he'd killed anyone. Glass bottles and silver dollar coins were fair targets, but sending a swarm of bullets through another man's chest was something most boys only pretended, when they played at their war games. Death places a burden on the living, and the killer himself bears the most weight. Even miscreants and murderers levy a stiff toll on a person for taking their lives. Hank started to moan and shake. Then like a rabbit released from a trap, he ran. Boots skidding through all that blood, streaking the floor. Dark footprints followed him out the door and into the unforgiving thunderstorm.

"Can one of you help me turn him?" I knelt beside Seth, his back blown open by the rapid departure of Hank's bullets. No one offered assistance. The young killer having departed, one man hurried past mumbling something about the sheriff. I heaved Seth over onto his back by myself. Closed his eyes so I wouldn't have to see his death gaze. He wore a rigid grin. His chest was a bloody ruin. My fingers tugged absently at the torn fabric of his shirt, and I recalled his good-natured complaining just that morning, as I'd helped him with the button at his collar. The doctor inside me battled through my impairments and made a fruitless examination of his wounds. Seth was plainly dead. No amount of surgical knowledge could undo that fact. The sound of my own blood roared in my ears, and I vomited beside the corpse. I'd seen my share of dead men, but it never got easier. I wiped my mouth with the back of my sleeve, felt Seth's blood hot against my face and recoiled.

Hank might be the one that shot Seth, but he was dead because of me. I was the one who brought us to Texas on this fool's errand.

I remained on my knees in the blood as all the cowards emerged from their hiding places and went about their frantic business.

Shouting for help. Trading descriptions of the young boy and his deadly pistols. It would not be long before everyone in town knew that a performer in *Cowboy Dan's Wild West Revue* had killed a man at the Silver Ace, shot him to death in cold blood. And no matter how I'd tried to reassure Hank, he would surely face consequences. A man claiming to be a doctor stood over the body for a few seconds, asked me questions I could not hear, then left, presumably satisfied that Seth was beyond his care. My head hurt, and I vomited again. People came and went as I remained on my knees, my hands on Seth's chest. Boots stomped through blood and long shadows passed overhead. People spoke, but their voices were ephemeral things, and I could hear nothing but the sound of my own panicked breathing. I knew I should be doing something, even if only to pray to the spirits that his soul find rest. But my wits and my wisdom had taken leave, replaced by a dull, skeletal intellect that could not parse the challenges of the moment.

After a time, someone knelt beside me in the blood. Placed a hand on my shoulder and shook awareness back into my mind. He spoke in a voice that I recognized.

"What occurred here, Catherine?"

"Aubrey. I am sorry."

"I don't require apologies," he said. "I want to know what happened to my brother. They say a boy shot him."

"Yes, a boy."

"Talk to me!"

He shook me again, and I finally opened my eyes to his face. Aubrey wore a mask of fury. Eyes red and tears streaking his handsome face. His teeth grinding together in a feral manner that unsettled me. I pushed back against the alcohol and the terror, reminded myself of the sort of man I was dealing with.

Something needed to be done to keep him from murdering Hank. For that would surely be his course of action, once the identity of his brother's killer was revealed.

"Help me stand, please."

Aubrey lifted me roughly to my feet. I noticed there were a dozen others standing over the body, all remarking on the amount of blood, and the sudden violence of the attack. Aubrey drew me away from the scene, toward the bar where he could have me alone.

"Tell me who killed my brother."

"The room was ill lit, and I am quite drunk," I said.

"I adore you, Catherine," said Aubrey. "But that doesn't mean I won't kill you. Can I assume it was our young friend, the Hurricane Kid?"

"Paying him back in kind with bullets will not restore your brother to life."

"No, that is your task."

"Aubrey, Seth is gone.

"That may be the case," he said. "But you're going to bring him back."

"Aubrey, I cannot."

Aubrey shoved me against the bar. My back struck the polished wood, and I started to slip, but Aubrey caught me by the arm, held me half suspended. My head spun, and I swore to any being that would listen that if I lived through this experience, I'd never drink again, never allow myself to become compromised in this manner. Aubrey lifted me toward him, pulled me so close that I could feel the burn of his beard against my cheek. He smelled of whiskey and his ever-present sandalwood cologne, but the stink of his sweat and his grief overpowered everything else. His fingers dug into my arm, like he meant to crush my bones.

When he spoke, his voice resembled the growl of a wild animal, and I wondered if Aubrey Dawson had revealed his true self to me for the first time. "You have cheated death before. I expect you to do it again."

Devoured By the West

Across the Bloody Frontier to Fort Ellis, Montana Territory
Autumn 1879

BY THE TIME I WOKE, Falling Bird had fashioned a crude travois from the bones of our broken wagon. I wiped away the blood and the mud from my eyes and saw that he'd strapped Frank to the contraption, along with what little remained of our supplies. A small canvas bag filled with soggy food. A jug of water. My leather bag, now lathered in filth. Blue skies prevailed, and the gray remnants of the storm were just visible far to the east. Frank was a bloody husk, but he was still alive. Unconscious, and blazing hot to the touch, but alive. He rested before me, a miraculous product of my stubborn desperation, and yet my miracle was tainted somehow. An undercurrent of uncertainty tugged at my once adamant resolve, and I could not yet identify what caused my change of heart.

Memories of the roaming Sioux who'd killed the others dampened Falling Bird's euphoria from the night before. Fort Ellis was a long walk, and if the Sioux were still close, they could ride down on us in open country and we'd both earn a bloody death. So, Falling Bird urged speed. He allowed me a moment to stretch and gather myself. Then he hefted the twin poles of the travois over his shoulders, and began marching out of the valley, dragging Frank behind him.

I followed, a sullen shadow.

Falling Bird was not a young man, but he moved with alacrity. After a few miles, I offered to assume the burden for a time, but he shook his head.

"I rode out here with him," he said. "The job is mine to bring him back home."

Frank still had not moved, apart from the steady rise and fall of his chest, and the occasional twitching of his blackened fingers. He stank of the grave, and I could not ignore the scavenger birds spinning circles above us in the forever blue sky.

"Do you know why he hasn't opened his eyes?" asked Falling Bird.

"No," I said. "My ritual is complete. From here on out, we traverse uncharted territory."

"But if we get him to the fort, he can be revived?"

"You're asking me questions for which I have no answers. He is alive. That's all I know for certain. What form that life will take remains to be seen."

"Dr. Prosper will have thoughts on how to further heal him."

"Dr. Prosper is a buffoon. I will be the one who heals him. If such a thing is possible. Have you forgotten I'm a doctor too?"

"I believe you're more than a doctor."

"You're finally willing to concede I'm not crazy?"

"I won't apologize for questioning you," he said. "You would never have accepted such wild claims without proof. Nobody would have."

"I might have believed the word of a friend."

"Not if it required you to suspend how you reckon reality."

"When tasked to choose between hard reality and nebulous

hope, I find there's little choice for me at all. Hope wills out."

"Well, your hope certainly prevailed this time," he said. "That much is true."

"Why must you continue to harass me?" I asked. "Did I not bring Frank back from the dead exactly as I claimed I would?"

"There's little doubt," he said. "But his condition is troubling."

There was no arguing that point. Frank's skin remained a pale green hue, and black corruption traced the paths of his scars. I could feel a sizzling sensation in the air as the magick continued its work, but blood still seeped from Frank's wounds, and decay continued to advance. Frank was once again ensouled, but what manner of physical form had I committed him to? Would the ritual overcome nature, and heal him fully, or would this piece-meal body become a prison from which his being could never escape? My belief in my own abilities had carried me this far, but these questions conspired against my happiness. Resurrecting my husband should have left me overflowing with delight, but instead I was haunted by doubt, and terrified of what I'd done.

And there was something else. Something I couldn't put my finger on. Apart from Frank's physical condition, I sensed another sort of corruption.

What caused that sensation, I could not say.

But I'd learned that such nagging thoughts were often messages from the universe. Either spirits trying to engage with me, or a sort of vast communal knowledge, native to the astral plane, endeavoring to make itself known.

Whatever the case, it was unsettling.

The going was hard, but when night fell, Falling Bird did not stop. Without a lantern to guide us, we proceeded in darkness. Sometime deep in the night, we slept for a few hours, but he roused me well before daybreak, and we resumed our arduous trek. Several days passed this way. My muscles ached and my feet grew blisters, but I didn't complain; Falling Bird walked the same path, carrying the weight of years and dragging Frank behind him, and he seemed untroubled by the effort. The wilding wind worked against us, always at odds with the direction of our progress, and a bone-deep cold settled across the land. We woke one morning to frost crusting the ground. A gray fog consumed the mountaintops, and sat upon the plain like a threadbare quilt.

Throughout our journey, my thoughts were consumed by shadows. Obsidian memories that stalked my daydreams and manifested in the real world as leering, translucent faces and willowy bodies that seemed to float alongside me, propelled by the wind, rather than moving of their own accord. Falling Bird did not perceive them, or if he did, he did not admit it. But they were assuredly creatures of substance, not mere dreams. There was no room for concentration. No environment where I might still my mind and discern their true nature. But it became evident to me as we delivered the fruits of my hubris back to Fort Ellis that I had removed more than Frank's soul from that other realm.

We rested the last night, less than fifteen miles from the fort. I waited for Falling Bird to sleep, then performed a banishing ritual. I told myself I didn't want to cause him further worry, but in truth, I was loathe to receive another dose of criticism. The ritual brought me peace and quiet, for a bit. But by morning, the spirits that had attached themselves to our journey returned, emboldened by my inability to keep them away for long.

Whatever disillusionment I felt about Frank's resurrection, these shadowy beings were the source. Their motives remained inscrutable, but their presence portended nothing good.

As we walked the last miles back to the fort, I daydreamed about Louisa Jupiter. I'd closed my mind to her guidance when

I'd closed my heart to her love, but I would listen now. If only she were there to counsel me.

Louisa was fond of saying *magick abhors haste*, and there was no doubt the shock of Frank's death had accelerated my actions to a dangerous pace. Louisa had taught me the proper ways to treat with spirits, but something in the death ritual had summoned beings with whom I had no desire to consort. Perhaps if I'd stopped to consider all possible outcomes of the ritual, I would have stalled my plans. Most likely not. Exactitude was a basic tenant of the Three Rose Temple, and no true adherent to their path would ever proceed with such an untried ritual without years of forethought and planning. That was always my weakness in their eyes. I would rather leap into uncertainty than wait for revelations that might never come.

Anxiety muddied my thoughts. Gray spirits swarmed like angry insects.

I walked a bit with my eyes closed. Tried to slow my breathing.

Memories of Louisa comforted me. Her calm voice like a ghostly whisper, explaining how to connect my conscious mind with my higher self. That same voice explaining how we must tune in to what our *unconscious* mind is trying to tell us. While the Three Rose Temple was the source of so much of my esoteric knowledge, it was Louisa who had started me down that path, and so much of my core understanding of magick had come from her. She made it seem so simple. Like universal truths accessible to all, not the shadowy, secretive endeavor it had become.

I imagined Louisa in her beauty, walking alongside us. Her dark curly hair, her wry grin, and her eyes that held back nothing. Montana was a lonely place, and I longed for her closeness and her guidance.

Falling Bird grunted with exertion as the land sloped upward.

He'd refused my repeated requests to pull the travois for a while, so I'd stopped offering.

Instead, I *listened*.

Perhaps Louisa and I connected somewhere on the astral plane, or perhaps my higher self was indeed trying to tell me something, but it felt as if she truly had joined us on our journey. My unwanted spectral companions faded into the gray morning. They would return, but in those peaceful moments, I believed Louisa was with me somehow. I couldn't see her, but her presence was as familiar to me as my own reflection. Tears streaked down my face as I followed behind Falling Bird. Frank still had not opened his eyes, but he continued to breathe. Continued to *live*. And I knew that if Louisa didn't agree with what I'd done, she at least *understood*. Her spirit walked beside me. Comforted me. Assured me that all was forgiven between us, and reminded me there were ways of dealing with unruly spirits, and methods by which any ritual could be undone.

If Frank could truly live, then no amount of haunting was too much to endure.

I would gladly become a ghost myself if it meant saving him.

But if I'd accidentally imprisoned Frank's soul in a dead body, I knew that Louisa would help me set it free.

Our arrival at Fort Ellis was met with little fanfare.

Dozens had ridden out to hunt down and punish the men who'd killed Frank and the others, and only a skeleton crew remained. We were able to convey Frank's still unconscious form to the medical building without close inspection, and we endured few questions.

Inside the hospital, we placed Frank's naked body on the bed, and I administered my poultice to his many wounds. During our cold passage, much of the damage had healed dramatically, and I could still feel the magick tugging at the air around him. But he remained as a man sleeping, unable to wake.

Corporal Levi appeared much improved. He sat upright in his bed, and watched me tend to Frank with a look of unveiled alarm on his face. The man who'd been unable to stop vomiting was deeply asleep, and he looked sicker than ever. He moaned and writhed and smelled of spoiled meat. Whatever treatment Dr. Prosper administered had not yet relieved his suffering. The doctor himself remained mercifully absent while I made Frank comfortable. But it was not long before he appeared in the doorway like a miniature storm, full of sound and fury.

"Where have you been, Dr. Coldbridge?" he asked. "And who is this man?"

"My husband, Frank."

"Well, I am sorry for your loss, but this corpse belongs elsewhere. We cannot expose our patients to the vapors of decomposition."

"I would not bring a corpse in here. Frank is alive."

"This man is clearly dead," he said.

"He *was* dead," said Falling Bird. "But his condition has improved."

Dr. Prosper was so taken aback by the sudden arrival of a dead man in his hospital building, that he seemed not to notice the Crow in his midst. I had more than once seen him refuse treatment to Indians on the grounds of *religious freedoms*, and to my knowledge, none had ever remained in the hospital for long without Dr. Prosper driving them away. He ignored Falling Bird, made a cursory examination of Frank. Fussed about with the poultice and mumbled to himself as he ran his fingers along the rapidly healing scars where the new limbs had been joined. Frank's dull green hue had grown lighter as we traveled; parts of him were transparently pale. I'd been working to clean him up when Dr. Prosper arrived, and he was still smeared with blood and filth. The stiches where I'd repaired him were black with rot. But his fingers continued to twitch. His chest rose and fell. And when Dr. Prosper placed his fingers at Frank's throat and found a pulse, he gasped.

"What is this?" he said. "What have you done to him?"

"Cannon fire ruined his body," I said. "We found him broken and I was obliged to put him back together with only the medical supplies I carried."

"You performed field surgery?" he said.

"Yes. I reattached his limbs."

"That's not possible," he said. "And these are not his limbs."

"Nevertheless, he is alive."

"Can you help heal him?" asked Falling Bird.

"I can do nothing for this man," said Dr. Prosper. "Save hold a pillow over his face until he expires. In his condition, it would be a mercy."

"I would recommend against that action." Falling Bird positioned himself between the doctor and Frank. He made no move to threaten the doctor, but his intention was clear.

"You are not welcome here," said Dr. Proctor.

"Escort me outside, if you are up to the task."

Unwilling to test Falling Bird's mood overmuch, the doctor turned his ire toward me.

"This thing you've done is sickening," he said. "You are grieving, I'm sure, but your husband is beyond medical help. You may have a carnival attraction, but you will never have a husband."

"He is healing. I can feel it."

"You can *feel* it?" said Dr. Proctor.

"It's not medicine that heals him," said Falling Bird. "It's magick."

Dr. Prosper snorted. "You're both mad."

There remained no reason to hide my true self from the doctor. Or from anyone, really. The thought of this odious man, treating me like an upstart child, too stupid or rebellious to accept his fatherly wisdom, became more than I could bear.

"You must open your mind, Doctor," I said. "Your self-righteous nature clouds your judgement."

"Leave this place," he said. "I won't be spoken to that way."

"Oh, I believe you will. I'll allow that you're an adequate doctor. Though perhaps not overly skilled, if these are the finest accommodations the Army could find for you. I am a woman, and they preferred me far away, where I could cause little trouble. What is your excuse? No matter, I've seen you do good work, when you can contain your need to belittle others and befoul every room with your unearned superiority. But there is hatred in you. You are fearful and small. Afraid of any person or any opinion that runs counter to your own. You would fare better in this world if you embraced a willingness to listen, and to learn."

"Young lady, there is nothing you could teach me."

"I'll not be referred to as *young lady*," I said. "You may address me as *doctor* or *magus*, take your pick."

"Magus?"

"Indeed. While you limited your studies to medicine, my education embraced more mysterious topics as well. I've cultivated talents that are beyond your simple worldview. You could never fathom my abilities. Your mind is locked up like a bank vault. Even the *possibility* of magick would leave a man like you shaken to his core."

Dr. Prosper laughed. "You want me to believe you saved your husband with witchcraft?"

"I don't care what you *believe*. The truth remains unchanged. I used magick to bring him back from the literal land of the dead."

Dr. Prosper took a quick step back. Followed that with another few steps. He kept an eye on me, like he'd suddenly realized I might be dangerous. I'm not so sure he was mistaken about that.

"Witches and Indians and monsters," he said. "This is a place of healing. There is no home for any of you here."

"I'm afraid there's very little you can do about it."

"Devils abound." Dr. Prosper moved toward the door, never taking his eyes off me, then hurried out of the hospital.

"Where do you think he's going?" asked Falling Bird.

"I haven't a care, as long as he remains there."

"He's not the sort to abandon a quarrel."

"If he returns to make trouble, we'll move Frank elsewhere. I wanted him in the hospital in case I need to employ any traditional medical care once he wakes. But I'm not certain that will be necessary. The magick is doing its work, and I don't think it needs any more help from me."

The air in the hospital smelled like the aftermath of a thunderstorm. Electric and charged with potential. The spirits that had followed me across the plains retreated to the corners of the room, fearful spectators in this final phase of Frank's resurrection. Whatever was happening was beyond my control now, but I could feel the weight of my magick pressing in on all sides. We would soon know Frank's fate, one way or another.

Frank's body shuddered, and when I placed my hands on his chest, I could feel his heart running like a racehorse. His skin was slick with sweat, and still burning hot to the touch. Falling

Bird brought me a towel and a basin of cool water, and I worked to clean him some more. There was little I could do until he either expired or regained consciousness, so I did everything I could to make him comfortable in the interim.

When Dr. Prosper returned some fifteen minutes later, he was not alone. Preacher Paul Meek followed in his wake, a look of frank concern on his young face. No doubt the good doctor had prepared the preacher for a scene of dancing devils and blood rituals, and he'd come outfitted for spiritual battle in his black vestments, clutching a Bible before him in both hands. With them was a soldier even younger than the preacher. Private Richard Bean was barely eighteen, a quiet boy, soft-spoken and always kind in our infrequent encounters. He was one of the few soldiers left behind at the fort, and looked uncomfortable as he followed the raving doctor into the hospital room.

"Witness the state of this poor man!" Dr. Prosper summoned Private Bean closer to Frank, expecting perhaps the boy would make a quick inspection of the body, and determine at once I was a witch in need of a pyre. Instead, he stood over Frank and grimaced. Put a hand over his nose to mask the stench.

"He's badly injured," said Private Bean.

"Badly injured?" said Dr. Prosper. "He is a corpse!"

"I'm no doctor," said Private Bean. "I don't know about any of that."

"A medical degree is not necessary to look upon a man who is green and black with infection, and determine he requires the services of a mortician."

Private Bean looked to be turning a bit green himself. He kept his hand over his face, and mumbled through his fingers when he spoke to me. "Dr. Coldbridge, this is your husband, isn't it? I'm sorry for his condition."

"Don't address her," said Dr. Prosper. "She is the wellspring from which this atrocity flows."

"I don't understand why you brought me here?"

"This woman and this savage have conspired to abuse a corpse. She claims to be a witch with the power to bring him back from the dead. The reason I brought you here, is to take them into military custody."

"Sir, I don't have authority over witches."

"This is not a joking matter."

"No, I don't think it is either. I'm just saying, I don't see that any crime has been committed, and my rank is not sufficient to arrest anyone here."

"Then at least dig a hole and bury this man. Get him out of my hospital!"

"Frank is alive," I said.

"Your opinion in this matter is of little value," said Dr. Prosper.

"That's unkind," said Private Bean. "I don't suppose you need to talk to her that way."

"Has she bewitched you, boy? Take this body and bury it somewhere!"

"Please don't do that, Private," I said. "As you can see, Frank is very much alive."

I felt it. I sensed it. I *willed* it.

Frank opened his eyes. Blinked. Coughed the death out from his lungs with so foul an odor that the young private gagged and had to turn away for a moment.

Frank began to moan, and we crowded around him. His body radiated heat.

"Your husband is alive," said Private Bean.

"That's what I've been trying to tell my colleague."

"He is destined for the grave," said Dr. Proctor.

"As are we all," said Preacher Meek, ever eager to remind us of our mortality.

Frank moaned louder, tried to sit. Private Bean leaned over, helped pull him up into a sitting position on the bed. Frank's eyes were glassy. Void of expression. Every shadowy spirit in the room came alive with glee, and they spun a whirlwind around us.

"Frank. Take your time. It's me. Catherine."

"Go easy, sir," said Private Bean.

Frank turned toward the sound of the private's voice. Raised his arms. Grabbed the private by his head with both large hands. The private tried to pull away, but Frank drew the boy to him.

"Let him go, Frank!" I said.

Falling Bird and I both grabbed Frank's arms, tried to release his grip on the private. But Frank had gained immense strength, and our efforts yielded no results. We might as well have wrestled with a stone statue. The spirits sang, and Frank's moaning became like a foghorn in the small hospital building. Dr. Prosper began howling about black magick and bloody death but his voice was swallowed by Frank's moaning and by Private Bean's screams as Frank wrapped an arm around his head, pulled the boy's face close to his chest, and began to squeeze.

The shadows shrieked.

Private Bean's skull cracked open with a sound like a massive tree branch snapping in half.

Frank dropped the dead boy to the ground.

Then he looked my way, and began to scream.

Frank rose from his hospital bed. He stood taller than I remembered him. Heavier, like a great lumbering beast. More screams tore loose from his throat, and he snatched out at me with one arm. I managed to sidestep and scamper away. Private Bean lay dead at Frank's feet, blood seeping from his broken skull and snaking out across the floor in red rivulets. Whatever I'd imagined Frank's resurrection to be, it wasn't this. The sudden shock of what he'd done left my heart racing and my mind alive with terror. Magick had never been something I was afraid of, but in that moment, it moved through the room like a furious storm, far beyond my ability to guide or control. The ragged edges of Frank's scars grew smooth as the magick coursed over him like a healing salve, but his eyes remained empty, and his movements seemed mindless.

Dr. Prosper had not stopped yelling. Frank turned toward the sound, arms outstretched before him.

Grasping.

There was something animalistic about Frank's nature. Movement and sound summoned his ire and drew his attention. He moved toward the doctor's voice. To his credit, Dr. Prosper positioned himself between Frank and Corporal Levi.

"Go away from this place, monster!" he said.

Frank continued screaming. He dragged his bare feet across the ground as he walked, streaking Private Bean's blood behind him.

"Frank!" I said. "Frank, come to me."

Frank moved slow, but he turned my way.

Preacher Meek moved beside me, stood ready to fend off Frank if he got closer. Falling Bird stood at my back. Their presence filled me with thanks and with shame. What had I done? Private Bean was dead, and Frank was a monster. No matter my intentions, the events unfolding were beyond my ability to stop.

Whatever happened now was entirely my fault.

"Dr. Coldbridge, you should leave," said the preacher.

Frank started toward us, still screaming.

"He's my husband."

"I don't believe this is really your husband."

We backed away, but the magick continued to work, straightening Frank's body and lending speed to his motion. One moment he moved slow as candle wax, then he lurched forward in a rush, put his hands around my throat and squeezed.

Preacher Meek grabbed Frank's wrist, tried desperately to free me, but my ritual invested Frank with supernatural strength, and there was no moving him. Dr. Prosper joined the fray. He grabbed a pine log from the woodpile near the iron stove, and struck Frank across the back with it repeatedly. All the while, the spirits sang dreadful songs and a violent white light passed behind my eyes and drew me down into the darkness. I could not even cough. No path remained for air to reach my lungs. I clawed at Frank's face, but my struggle was fruitless. Something cold and metallic brushed against my cheek. Falling Bird's pistol. He stood behind me, brought that weapon to bear just over my right shoulder, and pulled the trigger.

Nothing has ever sounded as loud as that gunshot.

Frank stumbled backward, hands coming loose from my neck. I dropped to my knees, gasping for air. Falling Bird stepped around me, fired twice more, putting both bullets in Frank's chest in a tight space with the first one. Frank tumbled to the ground, tried to stand. Falling Bird shot him again. Frank kept coming. Climbed back to his feet in a hurry, not overly troubled by the gunshots or the blood leaking from the holes in his chest. He never stopped screaming. Naked and crazed and relentless. By the time Frank was back on his feet, Falling Bird had his long knife at the ready. Brought it around in an arc meant to slice open Frank's midsection. But Frank was fast now. He caught Falling Bird's wrist, twisted it until it snapped.

The knife dropped, and Falling Bird howled.

He scampered back as Frank bent over and picked up the knife. Frank's eyes were still empty, but the uncanny force animating him palmed that knife like a natural fighter.

Dr. Prosper moved in again with his log, swinging. Frank avoided the strike, and the doctor fell off balance.

The log flew from his hands and clattered against the hospital bed where the vomiting man rested. He was wide-awake now, gray with sickness but animated by his terror.

Dr. Prosper regained his balance. Turned back toward Frank. Then that long-bladed knife crossed the doctor's throat with a sound like canvas tearing. Air whistled from the wound. Blood coursed down the doctor's chest like he wore a red bib. The doctor fell, and did not rise again.

Two dead now, because of me.

At that moment, Corporal Levi decided to affect his escape. He pushed back his blankets, threw his legs over the side of the bed, and attempted to walk. His bad leg was much improved, but still grievously injured. He managed to stand, to take a few unsteady steps. Then his bare feet found all that blood on the floor, and his legs went out from under him. Frank roared. He still held the knife, but did not bother to employ it. Instead, he stood over the fallen Corporal Levi for a moment, like an uncaring god considering his failed creation, then Frank began to mete out his vengeance with foot and fist. He stomped the man's chest, and hammered his face.

I should have done something, even if it meant my own death. But instead, I stood transfixed. Falling Bird's gunshots still rang in my ears, making every noise sound like it was travelling underwater. Still, I was not shielded from the horrible resonance of Corporal Levi's dying. Ribs snapped like kindling. Wet screams were unleashed, then cut short. Frank labored at his task with grunts and guttural howls. Falling Bird called my name, over and over, but his voice sounded so distant, there seemed no hope of reaching him. Corporal Levi was dead long before Frank stopped attacking, and somewhere on the edge of madness I couldn't help but think even a bone saw could not help the corporal now. Could not remove all the damaged parts and leave the rest of him hale and hearty.

When Frank finished, he turned my way.

Blood covered his expressionless face like a slick mask. He was lathered in the stuff, head to toe. My husband. The man I'd grown to love so very much. Nothing remained of that man, and thanks to me, his soul would never rest.

Frank would have killed me in that moment if Falling Bird hadn't lifted me bodily, and carried me out of the hospital.

I might even have let him.

Preacher Meek helped the vomiting man get outside as well, and we all trembled together in the cold sunshine, marveling at how quickly violence can steal our good intentions, leaving behind emptiness and death and mortal terror. Frank appeared in the doorway. The clamor had drawn the attention of a handful of confused soldiers. They fired at Frank, but of course their bullets were useless. Further enraged, Frank charged at the nearest man like a bull, bowled him over and began to ravage him with the long knife.

Every part of me ached with fear, and all hope escaped my body like air from a bellows. I ran. Gathered my black book and my medical bag from the wagon, then hurried to the stables where I located a saddled bay. Might be someone just rode the horse in from ranging, or one of the soldiers had been preparing it to ride out when the commotion at the hospital drew them away. It made no difference. I strapped my bag to the saddle and mounted the horse.

"What are you doing?" Falling Bird stood beside the horse, bloody and out of breath. Sounds of violence echoed across the parade grounds.

"We have to leave here," I said. "He can't be stopped."

"You can stop him. You *have* to stop him."

I laughed. It was an ugly sound.

"Don't you think I've done enough here? You would rely on my magick to undo this? You were right about everything."

"I can rely on nothing else," he said. "You built this monster. You must tear him down."

"No, I must go. You should ride with me."

"I had not thought you a coward," he said.

"Well, I suppose we are both learning new things about my character today."

I drove my boots into the horse's flanks, and he lurched into motion.

Falling Bird called after me, but I would not allow myself to listen. Perhaps I could have stayed and tried something. Made some attempt to reverse the ritual. But terror drove me from that place. Falling Bird was right. I'd revealed myself a coward. And in that moment, I embraced the new person I'd become.

My old self died there at Fort Ellis.

Though I continued to breathe, and my heart continued to beat, my life was over.

Forever after, I was a woman waiting for her grave.

Hard Promises

From the Morgue to the Silver Ace Saloon, Fort Worth, Texas
Spring 1905

AUBREY WATCHED as I repaired Seth's wounds.

The morgue was a single-story wooden building, conveniently located just behind the Silver Ace, a place haunted by shadows and the constant buzz of electric lights. A haphazard array of metal tables and half-finished coffins clogged the space, and the room was kept so cold with ice blocks that my fingers trembled as I removed the bullets from Seth's chest and sewed together the gaping holes. A congress of the dead attended the proceedings. A few who had presumably passed from some illness, and one man who'd snapped his neck and was forever looking sideways. The air was a mix of floral fragrance and chemical stench that burned my eyes. The mortician was a stooped, ancient man named Jep Carruthers who moved through the world like a clockwork toy, slowly winding down. He'd been reluctant to leave his post, but my wealth had proven more than adequate to buy his silence. Few advantages remained to me, but money was one of them. With a wet rag, I cleaned away the blood and the filth from Seth's body, grateful to be alone with Aubrey, so we might have a frank talk about the realities of life and death.

"I've tended to him, best as I can," I said.

"Thank you for that," said Aubrey. "Shall we proceed with the resurrection?"

"I've told you I'm not doing that."

"Oh, I believe I can convince you."

Aubrey had offered no further violence since our encounter in the Silver Ace, but I harbored no illusions about his willingness to do so. He occupied a chair in the far corner of the room, knees spread wide, one hand on his pistol hip and the other thrown across the back of the chair. His fine olive suit was a bloody ruin, and there was a wildness in his eyes that would have terrified me if I'd had any real desire to go on living.

"Kill me, if you want," I said. "It's better than being forever haunted."

The whiskey in my blood made me bold, but there was also the matter of my spectral tormentor. It swam overhead as I worked, frenzied and eager. So many of the other spirits, I'd managed to elude over the years, but this one never relented. I considered what Hank had said about a person being haunted by their own ghost, and I began to wonder if this last wandering spirit was some part of my own being, broken loose and gone feral. Others probed at the periphery of my mind, and the sheer amount of death and violence that had occurred in this place echoed through time, like a painful memory. Perhaps my skills had improved, and I could bring Seth back without consequences. Or perhaps I'd unleash every wicked soul that populated the Fort Worth afterlife. There was no way of knowing, and no way I'd risk a repeat of my earlier failure.

"I won't kill you, Catherine," he said. "But if you can't bring Seth back to me, I'll hunt down that boy and put him in a grave. You can be certain of that."

"Why should I care what you do with that boy?" I said.

"Oh, I think you care. Your heart is too soft."

"You really don't know me at all."

Despite his grief, despite his anger, Aubrey smiled.

"You are no mystery, Catherine. You're motivated by love and guilt, and I don't believe your conscience would allow that child to die."

"You aren't so mysterious either," I said. "You play at being the killer, but you don't have the nerve to point that pistol at me and pull the trigger."

Aubrey's smile never wavered, but he looked to be considering whether I was truly worth leaving alive. Before he reached a decision, the door opened, and two men walked into the morgue.

Frank came in first, dressed in gray wool trousers and a blue chambray shirt with the sleeves rolled up to his elbows. Scars and bruising marred his arms, but he wore a hat to cover his damaged head. He was so tall, he was forced to duck through the doorway, and I marveled again at the way my magick had stretched him out like a bit of saltwater taffy. An Indian man followed behind Frank, his brown face a tangle of deep wrinkles, his hair long and white down his back. He wore a fashionable black suit, tailored perfectly to his fit, and a flat top hat with a wide brim that hid his eyes in shadows. The two men walked in as if we'd been expecting them, and I supposed some part of me had been.

"I am sorry for what's happened," said Frank.

"Sorry your little friend killed him, you mean?" Aubrey kept his seat, but he appeared eager for violence.

"Yes, sorry for that."

"This was not Hank's fault," I said. "Seth was in a state of drunkenness. He initiated the conflict."

"Hank told me as much," said Frank.

"Perhaps you should summon young Hank to attend these proceedings," said Aubrey. "I'm keen to discuss the matter of his culpability, and the blood debt now owed."

The Indian man stepped up beside Frank. "I'm sorry about your brother. But you'll claim no retribution. That child will not be harmed."

Aubrey laughed, shifted in his seat so that both of his pistols were ready at hand.

"Catherine," said Frank. "You remember Falling Bird?"

And indeed, the shadows having lifted from his face, I recognized the man himself. He'd grown aged, but the fierce light in his eyes was the same. I rushed to hug him, drew him close for fear that he'd disappear like a banished ghost. Until that moment, I had no idea whether he'd lived or died at Fort Ellis, no confidence that he managed to elude Frank and escape the killing spree. Even my guilt about leaving him to die could not chase away my sudden joy. But when I wrapped my arms around him, Falling Bird remained stone-still. He did not return the hug, but stood quiet and implacable, neither welcoming my affection nor rejecting it.

I withdrew, deflated.

"You look well, Dr. Coldbridge," he said.

Nothing could have been further from the truth. The residue of my work colored my dress crimson, and I realized I'd soiled Falling Bird's fine clothes. Whiskey seeped from my pores and sweat coursed down my face. My hair was tangled, and blood dried beneath my fingernails. The direness of the situation had afforded me the clarity to repair Seth's wounds, but now my body felt heavy, and my head ached once again. Light-headedness claimed me. Vomit rose into my throat, and I fought back against the urge. I grabbed at the table where Seth lay dead, desperate to steady myself.

Aubrey began to laugh so hard at my discomfort, that it devolved into a wet, hacking cough.

We were drunken and disheveled. Reeking and foul.

There could not exist a more dissolute pair of humans on earth than Aubrey and me.

"I'm so sorry." My apology might have been for Falling Bird, or for Frank.

It really didn't matter which.

"Sorry means nothing, does it?" said Falling Bird.

"I suppose not."

He nodded. "We are all alive, at least."

"How are you. . ."

"I lured Frank from the fort. After you left. Mounted a horse and shouted after him. Coaxed him to follow. You recall his mindless state?"

"Of course."

"I kept a steady pace on that horse, just ahead of him. And he followed me for miles. Screaming. Until all the badness inside him burned out."

"Burned out?" I said. "What do you mean?"

"It was my intention to lure him into the wilderness so he could not find his way back. But instead, whatever demon possessed him eventually fled."

"Frank?" I said.

"I became myself again," said Frank. "Though I cannot explain how that happened. I would have told you earlier in the tent, but you departed in haste."

The weight of this revelation threatened to topple me, and I renewed my grip on the table.

Frank might not understand what occurred, but I could venture an educated guess. The violence he'd exhibited was a by-product of whatever force I'd called on to put his soul back in his body.

A side effect of the ritual.

Just a temporary reaction to the shock of leaving the land of the dead, and returning to our material world.

Frank had recovered himself no more than half a day after my departure. Had I remained with him, we might have enjoyed a lifetime together. I might have avoided decades of sorrow and regret.

But I'd abandoned him. I'd fled for my life.

Every ounce of my misery was well deserved.

"I'm such a fool," I said.

"I'm grateful you brought me back," said Frank. "Or I was for a very long time. Falling Bird helped me adjust to my new life. We have remained companions."

"This is a lovely reunion," said Aubrey, "but we have business to attend to."

I shook my head. "Aubrey, I refuse."

"What business do you mean?" asked Frank.

"Only the business of resurrection," said Aubrey.

"You want her to bring your brother back to life."

"Precisely so," said Aubrey. "And I'll entertain no arguments on the matter. You standing there before us in your hideous glory is testament to your lovely wife's powers. How can you deny another man the same gift you've already received?"

"We are not at odds in this matter," said Frank.

"Are we not?" said Aubrey.

"Surprisingly, our interests appear to be aligned."

"You're not serious," I said.

"We're not here to be sociable," said Falling Bird. "Our visit has a purpose."

Frank laid a soft hand on my shoulder, touched me for the first time since he'd had that same hand clenched around my throat in Montana.

"I'm sorry to ask this of you," Frank said. "But for Hank's sake, we need you to retrieve this man's soul."

I would have been less shocked if he'd told me he was leaving to live on the moon.

"For Hank's sake? What do you mean?"

"He is stricken by the matter. Felled by guilt. Hank is no killer. He is headstrong and cocky and rash, but there is a softness at his core. He's endured too much hardship in his young life already to have to take on something like this. The sheriff has already called on Cowboy Dan, eager to escort Hank to the gallows. We're a family, though. Nobody at the Wild West Revue would ever turn him in. Easy enough to spread the word he's lit out for the east. We'll do our best to keep him hidden for the duration of our stay in Fort Worth. We have a few more performances here yet, but then the show travels to El Paso. I would like for Hank to leave this place knowing Seth Dawson is alive."

"You, who have endured this atrocity," I said. "You would ask me to do that to someone else?"

"What have you done but given me new life?"

"I made you a killer."

"I suppose I was already a killer."

"Those were different circumstances."

"I'm not so sure," he said. "There are a great many dead Indians who can attest to my monstrous ways. Much to my sorrow and regret. Could be your ritual just enhanced something that was already inside me. But no matter the cause, those violent urges faded. The supernatural strength abandoned me. But the healing remains. *Life* remains. That's all that matters, I think."

"You'd have Seth go through what you did?"

"I don't care a thing about Seth," said Frank. "This is about healing Hank."

"And when Seth goes on a killing spree?" I asked.

"We can bind him," said Aubrey. "Keep him secured."

"How do you intended to do that?" I asked. "And how can you explain such a miracle if someone spots him, walking about, unharmed? Two dozen people prodded at his corpse. At least. Including the sheriff, the bartender, a couple of doctors, half the cowboys who ventured in from the ranches to waste their money. And the mortician. That old man is not so senile he can excuse the sight of a reanimated corpse."

"We can carry him into the wilderness," said Aubrey.

"Seth's soul is *here*," I said. "The ritual must take place *here*. There is no moving him out of town first."

"Consent to this thing," said Aubrey, "and I shall manage the logistics."

"And if it goes bad? If the wickedness does not depart?"

"You can reverse the ritual," said Frank.

"There is no reversal ritual," I said.

"Don't lie, Catherine," said Aubrey. "You explained to me before we even left St. Louis how this would work. If Frank couldn't be killed by traditional means, you would end his life with your magick."

"I would *attempt* it," I said. "Try to form some sort of spell from experience and hope. But that was always my last option. There is no verified ritual for removing a soul."

"But what if there was?" Frank pulled a folded piece of paper from his shirt pocket, handed it to me. The paper was wrinkled with age, and the ink smeared in places, but what was written there remained legible. The top of the page read *Untether the*

Soul. Below that, a whole list of things. Ritual elements. Correspondences. Notes on astrological conditions based on the time of the year. And a prayer to Hermes that countered my soul summoning spell.

The handwriting was familiar to me. Every loop and line, every sharp-angled letter.

The deliberate, precise scrawl of Louisa Jupiter.

"Where did you get this?" I asked.

"From a friend of yours," said Frank.

"How did she find you?"

Frank shrugged. "Same as you, I suppose. She tracked me with her powers. Hunted me down on the astral plane. Isn't that what you call it? This was some years back. Louisa found me in a Chicago chop house, and we shared an unsatisfying meal. Louisa talked a lot. Told me so much about you I never knew. About your relationship. About your *studies.* Things you never shared with me. I recall leaving that dinner feeling like you and me never really knew one another at all. But about this spell? Louisa wanted me to have it in case I ever reached the point where I grew tired of living. Said I could find you again, or find someone who would perform it. The prospect seemed laughable then, but I held on to it. I'm not sure why, but now I'm grateful to have it. Louisa knew I'd reach the point where I would want to die. And so, I have. Let that slip of paper serve as insurance against Seth's rampage, if needed. And then when that business is done, I'd like you to send me to the grave, where I belong."

I felt betrayed.

By Frank, by Louisa. By my own illusory hopes.

Whatever love Frank had for me was gone. Maybe it never really existed.

I'd loved Louisa too.

Would have sworn she loved me back.

But evidently, she'd kept track of my activities when I left the Three Rose Temple. Spied on me, even. Which meant she knew the mistakes I made, and the pain I loosed upon myself and others. Yet she never tracked me down to let me know things were okay. To let me know my husband was alive and thriving. Instead, she visited Frank, spilled all my secrets, and delivered him hope in the form of a spell.

Why was I so surprised? I'd abandoned everyone.

Why would any of them still care about me?

"Louisa . . . was she well when you saw her?" I asked.

"Yes, she appeared to be."

"And she said this spell would work? She's tried it?"

"She didn't say she'd used it, but she seemed confident in its efficacy."

"Her well of confidence was always overflowing."

"Catherine," said Frank. "I will beg if that's what you need me to do."

"I don't need anything from you," I said. "I'll do what you ask, just for the sake of concluding our business. I want nothing more than to take my leave of you all. And that includes you too, Mr. Dawson."

"Happy to oblige," said Aubrey. "Just as soon as Seth can walk out of here beside me, we shall catch the next train headed some-place better."

"I won't assume the guilt this time," I said.

"Guilt about what?" said Frank.

I'd lost years of my life in a black pit of regret. Torturing my-self over what I'd done. And those who could have soothed my soul apparently didn't care enough to let me know my guilt was unearned.

Could Frank really be so oblivious to my pain?

"Magick like this demands a toll."

"Whatever it is, I'll pay it," said Frank.

"You certainly will," I said. "Because I've already paid more than my share in this lifetime. Whatever we unleash with this ritual? The burden falls on someone else this time to make things right."

The morgue was an unsuitable place for the ritual, for fear that the lightning bolt attendant to the spell might wreck the building and burn it to the ground. So, we waited until deepest night, and relocated Seth to a flat bit of ground out behind the Silver Ace, a shadowed place bound on two sides by weathered fencing, and surrounded elsewhere by fat cedar trees. Not an ideal spot for privacy, but close enough to the death site to access Seth's soul. Frank and Falling Bird summoned the old cowboy Thirsty Picket, the sharpshooter Mabel Bones, and a few other trusted individuals from the ranks of the Wild West Revue, and they patrolled the perimeter, ready to challenge any who might approach the scene while I undertook the business at hand.

The fact that Frank trusted so many with the true secret of his death astonished me. I'd assumed he convinced most of the denizens of the Wild West Revue that his resurrection act was a parlor trick. But he explained that marvels and oddities were not uncommon in such travelling revues, and that truth was the only currency with which he intended to trade.

Over the years, I'd revisited the resurrection spell thousands of times, running my fingers over the words in the book, ruminating on what I might have done differently to affect a less horrifying outcome. This time, I made a few minor adjustments, but for the most part, the ritual remained unchanged.

Frankincense scented the night. My chants echoed through the empty streets.

And Hermes came to my aid, though with more reluctance this time. He attended me with a sense of unspoken admonishment, as if my will to overcome the natural order of the universe a second time was testing his patience. This would be the last time I'd bring someone back. I swore it. And so, he assented. Pulled Seth's being from the cauldron of souls and placed it back into his body.

When the lightning fell this time, I stood back, watched it lance through Seth's chest, pinning his soul forever to the earth.

Black smoke rose from his smoldering body.

But he was alive. I'd been granted another boon.

We should have moved Seth somewhere farther from watchful eyes, maybe hidden him out amid the chaos of the Wild West Revue, but Aubrey argued that his upstairs room at the Silver Ace was perfectly private and easy enough to guard, and I was in no mood to strike up another conflict with the man. Aubrey and Frank carried Seth's unconscious form up the rickety back entry steps that led directly to the hotel's second-floor landing, and managed to get him into Aubrey's bed without being spotted.

Rogue spirits crowded the room. No matter how hard I worked to keep them at bay, the ritual called to them like a train whistle on a cold night.

True to his word, Aubrey had considered on how best to bind his brother. He tied Seth to the bed with stiff ropes, then shoved a rag in his mouth to stifle any screams.

The deed being done, Frank and Aubrey heaved themselves into straight-back chairs on either side of the bed, and began their vigil. I paced at the foot of the bed, feet bare against the deep crimson rug, working to ground myself back in reality. Candles guttered in the dark room, casting a sheet of yellow light across the bed. Seth's chest rose and fell with steady breaths. I was exhausted, wanted nothing more than to huddle underneath a mountain of blankets and sleep forever. But anxiety propelled me. Rest would be hard to find until we'd weathered the storm of Seth's awakening.

"So, how long will this take?" Aubrey took a long drink from his flask, returned it to his coat pocket without offering any to me.

"There is no precise timeline," I said. "When I brought Frank back, he was out for several days. When he woke up . . ."

"You can say it," said Frank. "I'm not delicate."

"He raged for several hours, maybe half a day, if Falling Bird's memory serves."

"So, we have some time," said Aubrey.

"This is magick," I said. "Not science. There's no way to know for sure."

"I'll remain close for the duration," said Frank.

Despite his monstrous aspect, Frank's face was young and earnest, as if the years had not ravaged him the same way they had me. It was more than just the magick having forestalled his aging; it was a lingering naivete that should not have been there. And perhaps it was a sort of frail contentment. Jealousy moved through me like a cold flowing river. Frank had a family of sorts. Makeshift and odd, but a family. He had friends he could summon to his aid, while I could only command paid killers. I felt he owed all of this to me, and whatever guilt I'd been carrying for the hard life he lived evaporated. It was an ugly sentiment, but one I could not deny.

"Because we could not do this without you?" I said.

"Because I want to help," Frank said.

"Please don't lay claim to pure motives. Ours is a business transaction now, undertaken with or without your help."

"How have I offended you?" he asked.

"You haven't the power to offend me," I said. "I only long to finish all of this so I can be rid of you for good. You've haunted me for too long."

"How uncomfortable to eavesdrop on a lovers' quarrel." Aubrey continued to take healthy drinks from his flask, and I longed to yank it from his hand.

"Our time as lovers is long past," said Frank.

"Oh, I'm keenly aware of her status in that regard."

Frank studied the smile on Aubrey's face, as if he were taking the measure of the man for the first time.

I glared at Aubrey. "You're behind on current developments. Our ill-conceived dalliance has come to an end."

"But what a delight while it lasted."

"Hardly worth remembering, I'd say."

I'd had more than enough of Aubrey and Frank that evening. Without another word, I left the room and started down the stairs. My exhaustion was fierce, and I should have gone to bed, but I needed a drink to calm my mind and slow my charging heart.

To my dismay, Frank followed. Called my name. Caught up with me halfway down the stairs and followed me into the saloon proper.

"Frank, just leave me alone."

The Silver Ace was shadowed and empty. This was the dead, silent time just before daybreak. There was no bartender to serve me. There was no raucous horseplay to consume me for a time. Just a bitter quiet that felt heavy and interminable, like a grave I could never escape. Still, I made my way around the bar. Liberated a bottle of whiskey from the shelf and slaked my thirst.

"I'm not trying to upset your life," Frank said. "I don't expect anything from you."

"You expect *everything* from me!"

"I guess I haven't told you how grateful I am."

"Grateful? For turning you into this." I waved a hand at him, and grimaced at his distasteful appearance. It was a hateful thing to say. Maybe I was hoping Frank would get mad and leave me alone. Maybe I'd simply embraced my own meanness. Either way, Frank ignored the insult.

"Yes, for not giving up on me," he said.

"If you're truly grateful for this *life* I gave you, why do you want me to take it back?"

"I'm tired, Catherine," he said.

"Isn't everyone?"

"There is a hollowness in me. Nothing can fill it."

"Being dead is not a prerequisite for ennui."

"It's more than that. I'm aware of my own *wrongness*. As if the universe has a great eye fixed on my every action, and I'm constantly being judged unworthy. My existence feels like a violation."

"Hank is adamant that you keep on living."

"I know. And I love that boy. He's not my son, but we've grown close. The whole Wild West Revue, they're my family. I wandered a long time, trying to find my place in the world. People are unkind to someone who looks like a monster. But Hank and the rest, they love me. And that's kept me pushing forward for a while. But that love, it's never enough. No matter how much I want it to be. I'll find myself happy, on occasion, but the feeling never stays for long. Life has become something to endure, rather than to savor, and the prospect of it lasting forever is more than I can bear. You're the only person I know who might be able to remove my soul, bring me some peace. And so, I'm grateful that you loved me enough to bring me back to life, but I'll be more grateful still when you let me die."

"If you are so keen to die, why didn't you ask Louisa to perform the ritual?"

"Oh, I asked her," he said. "She refused me."

"Why is that?"

"She would not undo your work."

I took a seat at one of the tables, sat the whiskey bottle on top but kept both of my hands in a tight grip around it, like that bottle was the only thing left to ground me in reality. The room was dark. Slivers of creeping dawn moved in through the windows, but the morning remained too shy to show its full face. My ritual had conjured a lightning storm that brought with it dark clouds, and I suspected it would be some time before they departed.

Frank stood stiffly, hands in his pockets. His gray aura tugging at the darkness.

"Can you sit?" I said. "Makes me nervous when you hover there."

Frank complied. I wasn't certain what time the barkeep would arrive to begin another day serving watered-down drinks, or when the maid would come to toss the mattresses, but for now, it was just Frank and me, alone with our history.

"Things should not have gone this way," I said.

"Fate doesn't always leave us an option," he said.

"I don't believe in fate. Just our own choices and the price we pay for them. Please know, I did love you. I'm sure I did. And it drove me out of my mind when you died. Else I would have never been so reckless with my magick."

"I loved you too," he said. "Still do, I suppose."

"I don't love you," I said. "Not anymore."

"I'd not expect you to."

"I *am* sorry, though."

Frank shrugged. "Old wounds long healed. Wish you'd told me about your magick, though. You could have trusted me with that secret."

"It was never about trust," I said.

"Still, I'd like to have known."

"Magick is not likely what you think it is," I said. "For me, it's a spiritual pursuit. A way of connecting with something larger than myself, and maybe a way of doing some good in the world. Or at least that's how I used to approach it. Grand resurrections aside, most of my energy is directed at simple things. Understanding myself better. Divining truth and meaning from the world around me. Healing people. I can't escape from shackles, or make someone vanish. I can't produce a rabbit from an empty hat. Those are stage tricks. Prestidigitations. My magick is *real*. It's vibrant. It's beautiful and fierce and in many ways terrifying. But it's mine, and its secrets live in my heart. They aren't something I can share with you."

Frank watched intently as I spoke, and for a moment I recalled the beauty of his regard. The wonderful way I used to feel when his eyes were only for me.

"So, when Louisa said she wouldn't undo your spell, was it because she doesn't have the same gifts you do? Is she not as powerful?"

I shook my head. "None of this is about power. And Louisa's talents surely eclipse my own. This is about will. And in this case, about *willingness*. It's not that Louisa isn't skilled enough to undo one of my rituals. It's that she simply would not presume. Even if she disagrees with my choices, they are mine to make. And whatever mess I make is mine to fix."

"I spoke with her a long time," said Frank. "You two used to be friends."

"The very best," I said. "Until we weren't."

"But you never spoke of her, back at Fort Ellis."

"We were already broken by then."

"Might be you can repair your relationship?"

"If she wanted to reconnect, she could find me. She found you easy enough. She could have lifted my burden long ago, but instead she allowed my suffering to continue."

"I don't think it's like that."

"You don't know anything about it," I said.

"Louisa was forthcoming about your time together in school and in your magickal order. And about the full nature of your relationship."

"Frank . . ."

"All that was long before we met, and our life together is a distant memory. We have suffered enough, you and me. When all of this is over, and I'm dead, I'd like you to seek out happiness. Whatever that means to you in your present state."

Heat flooded my face, and melancholy caused my voice to hitch. "There's no happiness for me. No joy left to chase. Those times are long past."

"Did you love her?"

"Fiercely."

"More than you loved me?"

"That's a terrible thing to ask."

"You're right," he said. "I'm sorry."

"Frank, I'll never regret our time together. But I do wish I'd not left things how I did with Louisa."

"Then you should find her," said Frank.

"She might not want to see me again."

"Or it might be her fondest wish."

"If that was the case, she'd have come to me already. Louisa was never one to delay her desires."

Frank grinned, rearranging the map of scars on his face. Bathed in shadows, I could almost imagine his face as it had been in life.

"No," he said. "She certainly seemed a woman not easily deterred."

"She's a tornado in a tea shop."

We both laughed at that, and it felt good. Our voices echoed in the dimness of the morning.

"If you decide to track her down," said Frank, "just make sure you kill me before you go."

"I already told you I would."

"Yeah, you did. And I'm going to hold you to it."

Soul Reparation
From the Fort Worth Jail to the Afterlife
Spring 1905

BETWEEN DAYBREAK AND NOON, I managed a couple of hours of rest. When a knock came at my door, it roused me from a fitful sleep, and my chest filled with urgent terrors. Had Seth risen and overpowered Frank and Aubrey? Had he already sent half the souls in the hotel to an early grave? Bleary-eyed and exhausted, I wrapped myself in a blue cotton robe and hurried to answer the door. When I slid back the bolt and opened it, my caller was no one I expected. Mabel Bones stood before me, eyes red and weary.

Mabel was at least thirty years my junior, shorter than me but broad shouldered and strong. She wore an old-time prairie dress, green calico—her costume for the *Wild West Revue*—and rogue strands of blonde hair escaped from underneath her matching bonnet. Mabel's face was wide, her features soft, and she was a striking beauty. I hadn't known what to make of her during our brief meeting in Frank's tent, but the previous night, when she came to help guard the ritual, I'd found her to be a quiet and capable person. She called me *ma'am* like I was her mother, and posed no difficult questions about the resurrection. Mabel struck me as a steady bulwark against whatever chaos encroached, and so the sight of her standing in my doorway, shaking and on the verge of tears, only served to heighten my anxiety.

"Mabel, what's wrong?" I asked.

"They've arrested Hank."

"Who, the sheriff?"

Mabel nodded. Dabbed a tear from her eye with the flap of her bonnet.

"We had him hid away," she said. "But they came in the night. The sheriff. Some deputies. Whole bunch of men from the town. They tossed the entire camp. Tore down tents and beat a few folks in the process. A violent and vicious assault. We did our best to hold them off, but they would not relent. They dragged Hank out of there kicking and howling. Took him to jail. Ma'am, they're going to hang him, I think. You're the one seen what happened, so I thought you might could communicate the true circumstances of the shooting to the sheriff. I'd have gone to Frank, but he loves that boy so much, I'm afraid he'd march in there and murder someone. Cause more harm than good."

"Give me ten minutes to dress."

I closed the door, dug through my belongings to find a proper outfit that wasn't sodden or bloody.

When I finally walked down the stairs, into the saloon, Mabel stood beside the swinging doors, waiting for me, her Winchester rifle clutched in her hands.

"I doubt the sheriff will take kindly to you marching into his office with that rifle," I said.

"I'll surrender it if they ask," said Mabel. "Until then, I'm going to hold on to it. You didn't see the way they fell upon us. He might be the sheriff, but he's a bloody man."

I nodded. "Okay then, let's go."

Gray clouds lay flat overtop the streets of Fort Worth. My head still swam with alcohol, and I proceeded at a slow pace, so as not to reveal any infirmity. The jail was only a couple of blocks away, but the midday heat and the flurry of people moving along the sidewalk hindered my pace, and dizzied my mind. Mabel proceeded like a woman on a mission, clearing a path through the crowd, so I followed close behind her, bile in my throat and heart jumping like a bullfrog beneath my ribs.

There was nothing I wanted more than to be finished with these people and this place for good. To ride out of town and find somewhere to while away the last miserable years of my broken life. But it seemed every move I made led me deeper into a morass of guilt and responsibility.

I was unsure whether I'd ever escape.

The jail was a squat stone building that kept the cool air inside, and when we entered, it seemed far more comfortable a place than it had any right being. Electric lights hummed and a few men sat at sturdy desks, laughing at some joke as it faded away. The windows were thrown open to allow the breeze to move through, and the room smelled like fresh coffee and cedar trees. A pot sat on top of a small cookstove, the source of the coffee smell, and the sheriff himself, a man named Bramlett, was frying eggs in a skillet when we walked in. Sheriff Bramlett had questioned me to the point of exhaustion when he was summoned to the site of Seth's shooting, and I don't believe either of us left that meeting with a high opinion of the other. When we walked in, he turned a scowl our way and clattered his skillet against the stovetop.

"Get that rifle out of here," he said. "Less you want me to take it from you and add it to the collection."

A host of rifles, pistols, longbows, and assorted knives occupied a glass-front cabinet on the far side of the room, and Sheriff

Bramlett motioned toward it with a long fork he'd been using to flip the eggs, to demonstrate the Winchester's possible fate.

"I don't have anywhere to put it," said Mabel.

"Take it back to where you got it, and you can stay there with it," he said.

"I'll just lean it right here." Mabel let the rifle rest on its butt, the barrel leaned up against the doorframe.

"Why are you women here?"

"We've come to assess the condition of Hank Abernathy, the boy you arrested."

"The man-killer, you mean."

"Sheriff, I believe we talked over this at length. The boy defended himself. He'd be dead if he hadn't pulled his gun."

"I'm surprised you remember that conversation at all," said Bramlett. "Drunk as you were. You appear not to have sobered much, though some hours have passed. We frown upon public drunkenness around here, Dr. Coldbridge. You might ought to return to bed."

Sheriff Bramlett did not hide his amusement. He stood over the stove, white shirtsleeves rolled up, black pants tucked into his boots, his matching suit coat hung over the back of his chair. He wore his beard clipped short, and his face would have been handsome if not for his lopsided nose. Bramlett looked like a man who'd been kicked in the face by a horse, and refused to set the bone right. But when he grinned, his teeth were nice and even, white as pearls.

"I haven't been drinking," I said.

"Forgive me if I don't believe you."

"Hank doesn't deserve to be here."

"Hank deserves all of what he gets," said Bramlett. "Close to a dozen men saw him pull his pistol and kill that fellow. Saw the kid draw and shoot first, mind you. So fast the poor old boy he shot never had a chance to clear his holster. You might swear one thing, but there's plenty more will swear different. And you can be sure, soon as we get that boy up in front of the judge, he's bound for the gallows."

"You're a mean bastard, ain't you." Mabel's face was still red and swollen, but her tears had dried up, and a smoldering anger had banished her earlier fear.

A couple of the assembled deputies pushed back their chairs, made to stand, but Bramlett waved them off.

"Yes, I sure am," he said. "Especially when dealing with your sort."

"And what sort is that?" asked Mabel.

"People of low character."

"You judge people before you meet them?" she asked.

"Don't think I don't know all about you, Mabel Bones. And the crowd you used to run around with. I've seen your face on a wanted poster a time or two."

"That was a long time ago."

"Not so long I've forgot."

"What's any of this have to do with Hank?" I asked.

"It's the whole mess of them folks, coming into town. Some fools enjoy these revues that pass through, but I ain't one of them. Way, I see it, they're travelling bands of miscreants, half of them on the run from the law. Shiftless lazy actors. Outlaws too old to rob banks anymore. Dancing women with loose morals. Horse thieves and ruffians. And worst of all, a whole bunch of them red Indians. Roaming the streets of my town like they're welcome here. Might be folks have made friends with them savages elsewhere, but I refuse to forget all the murdering and scalping they done. All the women and babies they stole. They parade around, bold as brass, and put on a show. And we put good money in their pockets for the privilege of watching. No, I won't be part of that. And I won't look kindly upon any who travel with such devils, including that wild little boy back there in the jail cell."

My instinct was to argue with Bramlett, ask him what sort of atrocities he might commit, if strangers moved in and destroyed everything he held dear in the world.

But I took a breath. Steadied myself.

There was no winning an argument with him, and escalating matters would not help Hank.

"Sheriff," I said. "May I at least see him?"

Smoke rose from the sheriff's skillet, and the grease popped and hissed.

"God darn. Now you made me burn my eggs!" Bramlett slid the egg from the skillet onto a plate. "Yellow's hard as a rock, and I like mine runny."

Mabel had her hand on the barrel of the rifle, like she was thinking on what she could do with it.

"Keep your distance from that gun, girl." Bramlett pointed his fork at her, and put a hand on the pistol at his hip.

Mabel put her hands up, smiling. "Why I'd never think of shooting you."

"You might think about it," he said, "but you'd be dead before you put the plan into action."

"Sheriff," I said. "About Hank. Can I see him?"

"You can. I ain't so hard I won't let a doomed boy console himself with some company. Go on back there to the cells. But just you. I'm not so sure the outlaw Mabel Bones is quite as reformed as she claims. She's liable to try and bust him out of jail. Best if she stays where she is."

"I appreciate it, Sheriff," I said.

A row of cells spanned a long hallway off the main room of the jail, and all were empty but two. One held a sleeping man with no shirt on and a long white beard, and he snored louder than Gabriel's horn. The last cell at the end of the row is where I found Hank. He sat on the edge of a wooden cot, leaned over reading a book. When he saw me approach, he put a finger between the pages to mark his place. There were a couple of chairs scattered haphazardly in the hall, and I dragged one over to Hank's cell so I could sit and talk with him through the bars.

"I told you they'd hang me," he said.

"You did," I said.

"Nobody's fault but mine, though."

"You were defending yourself."

"They don't care about none of that."

"No, you're right. They don't. What are you reading?"

Hank showed me the cover of his book. It was a slender black and brown volume with a tall man on the cover, his face shadowed, smoking a cigarette. Blue and green scales covered him head to toe, like he was some sort of fish on two legs, and a fish he might have been, for he waited defiantly on a beach while a terrible storm swirled about. Two children stood on either side of him, one holding each of his large hands. A young girl, grinning like she was half mad, pigtails dancing in the gale. And a skinny little boy, sullen and grim, carrying a pistol so large one wondered how such a slight child could even lift it. Dark rain clouds colored the sky behind them, and towering waves prepared to crash down and swallow them whole.

The title ran across the top of the book cover:

THE LEGEND OF CHARLIE FISH: A TRUE AND ACCURATE ACCOUNT OF THE DEADLY TEXAS HURRICANE

"Is it any good?" I asked.

"It's all right. Not long on the truth, though. I've recognized quite a few historical inaccuracies."

"Do you read a lot?"

"No. Only when I'm really bored."

"Have they treated you well?" I asked.

"Well enough. Though they let a preacher come back here to harass me earlier. In my experience, when a preacher involves himself in matters, things begin to deteriorate in a hurry."

"What did he want?"

"He wanted to pray over me, on account of my imminent demise. He was concerned my soul might not be prepared for Paradise."

"Your soul's not going anywhere yet."

"They can hang me, I guess," he said. "But I'm not sure if it would take. Don't forget my mother's nail. Long as I have that in my shirt pocket, I'm not sure death is even possible for me."

I leaned in close, whispered to make sure no eager ears were listening from the other room. "We aren't going to test that theory. You aren't going to hang. I won't let it happen."

"You going to cast a spell to get me out of here?"

"It doesn't work that way."

"You can bring a fellow back from the dead, but you can't get me out of jail?"

"Not with magick. But perhaps by more conventional methods."

"You're going to break me out?"

"If needs be. But the way I see it, they can't hang you for killing a man who's still alive."

"So, you gave in to what Frank wanted?" Hank regarded me with a sour expression that left no doubt as to what he thought about bringing Seth back from the dead. "I figured you might have. That preacher asked a whole lot of questions about where

Seth's body ended up. The undertaker says it's gone missing, and the preacher is keen on making sure Seth gets a Christian burial."

"Won't be anyone to bury."

"Frank thinks he's helping me, having you do this thing. But he's not. I told him that, but Frank isn't one to listen."

"I did bring him back," I said. "Or I'm working on it, at least."

"I wish you hadn't. I would sure like Seth to be alive, I mean, but having experienced a resurrection of my own, I can tell you he is not destined for a happy life."

"I'm not sure how happy he was in the first place."

"I'm talking serious," he said. "Those of us who come back, it's like we're walking outside the real world some days. Life can be grand, on occasion. But our existence works against the natural order of things, and death is always calling. There is never a moment where it's not whispering in my ear. Seth ain't my favorite person, but I wouldn't put that on him."

"The man tried to kill you," I said. "I wouldn't cry too many tears over his fate. The way I see it, if we present him, living and breathing, to Sheriff Bramlett, he'll have no choice but to release you, straight away."

"No, I don't believe he will," said Hank. "That sheriff is a mean one. He won't let this affair pass without a hanging. He'll assemble some story to suit his needs. Say the man you brought is Seth's twin brother or something. Everyone saw him bloody on the ground. There's none can deny that. So, you'd have to convince the sheriff that you truly brought Seth back from the dead. And if you managed that, well I guess he'd gladly let me go, so long as he could slip the noose around your neck instead. Hang you for witchcraft."

"I'm not a witch."

"You think he knows the difference? You think he cares?"

"No, I suppose not."

Hank nodded. "There you go."

Hank was right. He'd thought about this from more angles than I had, and the prospect of Sheriff Bramlett's willful ignorance seemed the likeliest outcome.

"So, it's to be a jailbreak, then," I said.

Hank grinned. "Never broken out of jail before. Are you ready to spring me now?"

"Not yet," I said. "We need to wait for Seth to recover all the way first."

"How long will that be?"

"Can't say for sure. Not more than a couple days. But once he wakes, we're all going to have to leave town in a hurry."

"Just don't leave without me."

"Hank, I promise you I won't."

"Try to hurry things along if you can," he said. "I don't think the sheriff is one to delay his satisfaction for long."

Hank returned to his book, and I rejoined Mabel and the others in the jail office. Mabel and the sheriff seemed not to have stopped arguing during my absence, and they hollered back and forth at one another, voices full of spite. The assembled deputies sat grinning at their desks, content to let their boss take the brunt of Mabel's anger.

"Y'all broke John Brewer's arm when you attacked us."

"That red bastard with the big ears?" said Bramlett. "Lucky for him we stopped at his arm."

"Don't none of us deserve that sort of treatment."

"Y'all deserve that and more. Be thankful that boy is the only one we arrested. Probably should have hauled in you and a few others to boot. Not too late to fix that mistake."

"You ain't arresting me," said Mabel.

THE UNKILLABLE FRANK LIGHTNING

"Keep moving your mouth and I damn sure will."

"No need for that, Sheriff," I said. "We're leaving."

"I would advise you do so at once," he said.

I grabbed Mabel's Winchester, put it in her hands.

"Don't forget your rifle," I said. "You'll have need of it before long."

That night, Louisa found me in my dreams.

After our visit to the jail, Mabel and I took a shift at Seth's bedside. He still stank of death, but the steady rise and fall of his chest, and the flutter of his eyes behind closed lids signaled his body's ongoing repair, and we braced for the moment when he awoke and gazed upon the world anew. My spectral companion floated directly beside me, occasionally leaning over to study Seth, as if sharing my interest in his condition. More and more, I'd begun to question what sort of being haunted me, and to believe it was a part of myself. Not a creature stalking me for nefarious reasons, but a fractured bit of my own soul. This development offered little relief. That nature of the haunting might change my perspective, but all possibilities were equally disconcerting.

Mabel talked incessantly, outlining plans for how we might break Hank out of jail, and her ongoing efforts to keep Frank from marching there to murder everyone. She detailed the unkind treatment doled out by Sheriff Bramlett and his posse on the denizens of the Wild West Revue, and mapped directions for our flight once the time was right to go. She included me in every part of the plan. Somehow, I'd been drawn into their collective, and circumstances pulled me along like a tired wagon behind a team

of spirited horses. I had only come here to undo a wrong. I had
not anticipated the complexities inherent in my arrival, or the at-
tachments they would engender. I owed Aubrey his brother's life.
I owed Frank a death. And I owed young Hank his freedom. My
debts continued to compound, and the prospect of payment was
swiftly becoming more than I could bear.

When Aubrey showed up to relieve me that evening, I hurried to my room and crawled into bed, bone-tired and eager to
escape the world. I lay awake in the dark for a time, considering
all the vile people I'd encountered during my stay in Texas, and
wishing them ill. Purveyors of sorrow and pain. People who
wielded misguided morals against the poor and the unfortunate
and the *different*. The undertaker we'd paid for his discretion had
summoned the church and the law. The men in charge of finding
justice closed their ears to truth and hung men for sport. They
executed their duties with violence and mirth, comfortable in
the righteousness of their office. Unchecked and unquestioned.
Without a doubt I was the chief villain in their narrative. Had I
not brought a pair of hired killers to their town? By their reckoning,
was I not engaged in the ancient and evil practice of witchcraft?
They would never understand it was love and remorse that drove
my actions, for those emotions were as distant to them as the
moon and the stars and the planets.

These were the uncomfortable thoughts that consumed me as
I drifted to fitful sleep, and dreamed myself into the great hall of
the Three Rose Temple.

I'd not dreamed of the place in years. I'd not stepped foot there
in decades.

But Louisa remained. Waiting for me.

She occupied one of the overstuffed crimson chairs that lined
the perimeter of the expansive circular room. I lazed in a similar

chair opposite hers. Golden candlelight shimmered along the walls, and a large summoning circle lay between us, arcane geometry scrawled into the floor and illuminated with uncanny light. Stained glass windows were stationed at the north, the south, the east, the west, and dim light filtered in through scenes of elemental forces in furious motion. The walls were stone and the roof formed a silo far overhead, and every small sound echoed through the chamber like ghost song.

The place smelled like a bygone era.

It smelled like home.

Louisa looked not so much older than the last time I'd seen her. Long black curls fell across her shoulders, without a hint of gray. A red robe covered every soft angle of her body, and my heart leapt into my throat at the sight of her. For whatever disdain existed between us now, she was someone I used to love. She was *Louisa*. And it had been so very long since we'd faced one another in the waking world or in the vastness of our dreams.

"I wasn't sure you'd ever fall asleep." Louisa sat with her bare feet flat against the cold floor. She wasn't exactly smiling, but something about our meeting obviously amused her.

"You've been waiting for me?" I asked.

"Yes, for quite a long time."

"I would have come any time you called."

"Would you have?" she asked. "That seems unlikely. The way you left, there was little doubt how you felt about me. You were never truly happy in those days anyway. Probably best that you sought out another path."

"I had happiness," I said. "*We* had happiness. Not that it mattered."

The coldness of the dream world settled into my body, and I began to tremble. This was a wildly lucid dream. There was no distinguishing this astral version of the temple from the actual place. The air was heavy and wet, and the arms of my chair were rough with age beneath my fingers. I knew how it would feel to kneel and place my forehead against the smooth stone floor. I could hear the whining sound of the great door on the other side of the building, every time it opened and closed.

Louisa sat upright in her chair like it was a throne, her hands in her lap, her fingers drumming with nervous tension. "I should have helped you. But I can't change things. And I didn't come to argue about old times."

"We have nothing to discuss but old times."

"No. We have the *here*. We have the *now*. And though I may have failed you once, I don't plan to do so again."

"You didn't fail me," I said. "Your counsel was sound. It took me a long time to understand that."

"Yes, but when it became apparent you were unwilling to change course, I should have helped you. I should never have stood in your way. I'm so very sorry."

Her apology shook me. No matter how many times I'd imagined a reunion between us, I'd never considered Louisa having a change of heart.

"But that's not why I'm here," she said. "And we haven't unlimited time."

"Louisa, where are you? In the real world, I mean."

"Nowhere you can find me."

"I don't believe that," I said. "Seems like you found me easy enough, once you put your mind to it."

Louisa laughed. "Oh, I've followed your travails with great interest. You might have left a long time ago, but I never lost track of you."

"And yet, you never came to me."

"I assumed you'd not want me in your dreams. The way we left things between us."

"I don't mean in my dreams; I mean in the flesh."

"That's something I can't manage."

"Why not?"

"I'm dead, Catherine," she said. "I've been dead a long time. You are well acquainted with death. It's a wonder you never sensed it."

Of course, she was dead.

Her words unlocked the truth of it.

Louisa's death was something I understood in my sleeping soul, if not in my conscious mind. Never had she answered my desperate need throughout the years. Never had she weathered the stormy seas of our broken relationship to rescue me from my drowning life. But Louisa wasn't capable of hate. There was not enough enmity in the world to dissuade her from saving someone she loved. I'd blamed her for so many of my ills, but of course none of my failures belonged to her.

How long ago had Louisa died, and what had happened? She'd lived long enough, presumably, to meet Frank and to deliver her spell to him.

Maybe she'd intended to come to me then.

Maybe she died on her way to find me.

But the circumstances of her death were immaterial. Louisa was beyond my reach forever. Our chance to mend all we'd broken was gone and would not return.

Tears ran hot down my face.

"Louisa, I don't know what to say."

"I don't require you to say anything. My death is not a recent development. I finished mourning myself ages ago."

"Why do you linger here?" I said. "Is there nothing beyond this life that calls you?"

"Death is a mystery I shall not solve for you," she said. "But I am here now because we loved one another once. And I still consider you a friend."

"I could use a friend," I said. "My circumstances of late are dire."

"More dire than you imagine, I think."

"I have never lacked for imagination."

Louisa smiled then, and looked at me in a way that made me think of times long past. The smiled faded in a hurry, reminding me those times would not come again.

"Your position in the world is precarious."

"And forever has been," I said.

"Don't make light of this. You're in a difficult situation, and I don't believe you realize how bad it truly is."

"So, tell me."

"Your enemies are fond of killing. They will not be deterred. You've ventured into dangerous territory here. Violence resonates through this land like a dark song, and it weakens every man with an ear for such things. Men inclined to meanness and the infliction of pain. They lose inhibitions. Most days they shine with a veneer of respectability, but they'll not resist the killing urge when circumstances afford them an opportunity. So many people, they're only looking for an excuse. You understand this? Catherine, you can't underestimate the people around you. Your enemies, or your friends. The line between life and death is thin as parchment for everyone involved, because you made it that way. Violating the laws of existence. It's like you've unsettled the earth beneath everyone's feet, and now the fault line is ready to shift. I'm not saying that excuses what these people are about to do, only that your arrival and your latest ritual are all the justification they'll require to become the people they want to be. Do not hesitate to defend yourself. For they will not hesitate to put you in the grave when the time comes."

In the manner of dreams, Louisa was seated across the room one moment, then suddenly kneeling before my chair on the hard stone floor, her hands on my knees, eyes turned up to study mine, like she was trying to understand the desperation inside me that effected my sorry state. Astonished at her closeness, I allowed my hand to drift toward her, my fingers to move through her hair, my palm to press against the warmth of her cheek. She couldn't be dead. Not really. She was *right here*. But I was not so ignorant nor innocent to fool myself for long. This was still a dream. Louisa possessed no more substance than the echoey walls around me. Her touch was ephemeral, her affection a fleeting illusion.

"I can't stop Seth's resurrection now," I said.

"No, you can't," she said. "You paved that road, now you must walk it."

"Have you visited only to define my limited options?"

"No, I'm here to help you. I'm here to put you back together again."

"That's quite the task."

My hand remained on her cheek, and her hands remained on my knees, as if both of us were afraid the other would vanish.

"You are haunted," she said.

"Yes."

"But you've begun to understand the reasons for it. Your tormentor is a creature of your own making. A piece of yourself that you've lost. When you brought Frank Humble back from the dead, it broke you. As I warned you it would."

"I haven't forgotten my failures."

I pulled my hand away from her face, angry at her reproachful tone, but she clutched at my arm. Pulled herself closer.

"Our souls are fragile," she said. "But they can be repaired. I can help you."

"You're a ghost, Louisa. What can you do?"

"You should know better than most. Our existence transcends death. There's a spell to repair your soul. I mean to cast it, here and now. Whether I'm living or dead is immaterial to its efficacy."

"If that's true, why didn't you come to me sooner?"

"You weren't ready to listen. I tried over and over to call you, in recent years. Maybe you weren't quite broken enough? That sounds terrible, I know. But you're so close to me now. That broken part of you longs to be in the afterlife, whether you know it or not. That's why we can interact with such clarity. But you still have a life, even if you don't think it's worth living. And once you're healed, I'll be truly a ghost to you. At least until your life is finished, and you join me here. Assuming that's your will when the time comes."

"I can't say whether it will be or not," I said.

"That's okay," she said. "You have plenty of time to figure things out."

Louisa lay her head in my lap and began to chant, her voice high and erratic, rising and falling in volume until finally it assumed a steady cadence, and I knew she'd found the heart of her spell. I stroked her hair. Leaned close and buried myself in the remembered scent of her. Her words worked to fill the emptiness inside me. I began to sob. I wept for the love we'd had. Wept for everything more we'd never have. There was no telling what might have happened if I'd stayed in Philadelphia. If I'd forgiven Louisa and worked to forge a life together. We'd never know. But I imagined a world where Frank found a woman who carried him far away from Fort Ellis, and loved him for the rest of her life. Of a world where Aubrey and Seth Dawson never met the woman who delivered them to a world of ruin. And most of all, a world where Louisa and I could have found happiness together.

Everything could have been so much easier.

As the spell progressed, we became untethered from the environment, alone together in a vast darkness. Life and death danced around us.

Louisa's chant became a whisper.

Shattered pieces of my soul flowed slowly back into my body. Refreshing as cold rain. I gasped. Laughed in spite of myself. In this place of the dead, I felt suddenly more alive than I had in years. Joy suffused my thoughts. And *hope*. Perhaps there was a way to bring Louisa back, once I'd become fully healed. A way to make right all that had gone wrong. Then Louisa grew insubstantial to my touch, and I understood that life was carrying me away from her again.

Illusion has such a power to enthrall, especially when it tempts you with things that can never be.

"What happened, Lousia?" I asked. "How did you die?"

Louisa began to fade; smokey tendrils of her being chased away into the deep darkness.

"Does it matter?" she said.

Suddenly it mattered very much. My desperation to know what happened, to understand her fate, was so enormous that the fear of never knowing terrified me.

But it was too late for all that.

Louisa was gone.

Thunder rumbled from every direction, and lightning cut a silver path across the horizon of my dream. Even in this place, the storms would not relent.

The thunder began a persistent hammering, and I could feel the low sound of it, resonating in my teeth.

Then I sat up in bed, awake. Crying and gasping for air. Violent rain fell outside, and someone knocked frantically at my door.

"Go away!" I said. "Leave me to sleep."

"Let me in, Catherine!" Aubrey's voice was a threadbare rasp, as if he'd been yelling a long time.

"Leave me be, Aubrey!"

"He's awake!" said Aubrey. "I need your help. Seth is awake!"

Summoned by a Witch

Inside the Silver Ace, Fort Worth, Texas
Spring 1905

SETH STRUGGLED against the ropes binding him. Already they'd begun to loosen and fray. Frank leaned over the bed, grappling with Seth, trying to hold him down. Thirsty and Mabel battled against his kicking feet. By the time Aubrey led me into the room, Seth had managed to wriggle one leg loose, and was working to throw it over the side of the tiny bed. He'd chewed through the rag in his mouth, and his animal howls resonated in the cramped room. The old undertaker, Carruthers, stood by the window, moaning like a lost soul, and I knew his presence could not portend anything good.

"How do we keep him still?" Aubrey hurried to join Frank in the fight to keep Seth from snapping the ropes.

"You'll recall I told you this was a poor place to bring him," I said.

"My memory is fine," he said. "I'm asking for help."

"His strength is immense," said Frank.

"As I reminded you all it would be," I said.

"Strong as a team of mules," said Thirsty.

"We'll just have to keep him held down until the violence

burns out. That's the way it worked with you, Frank. That's what you said?"

"Yes, but it took several hours," said Frank.

"Then I hope you gentlemen do not tire easily from your efforts."

Seth's resurrection should have terrified me. Should have summoned memories of Frank's bloody attack, and the loss of my old self. But I was entirely at peace. Seized by a sort of wild euphoria that drew the world around me into sharper focus, and left me with a feral smile on my face. Laughter threatened. My body trembled with life. And though rogue spirits circled the hotel room like stalking beasts, my spectral tormenter was gone. She was back inside me now. Her presence made me whole again. And for the first time in so many years, I couldn't feel an emptiness, yearning to be filled. No gray fog of guilt coloring my thoughts. There remained only a true and transparent understanding of the world around me, and a renewed connection with the whole of the universe.

My thoughts were clear. My resolve certain.

Was this the person I used to be, before meddling with death ruined my life?

"What manner of creature are you?" Jep Carruthers was bent and thin with age. He looked like a stickman in a dusty black suit and lopsided string tie. He arranged his drawn face into the approximation of a scowl, but there was no mistaking the fear in his eyes. Or his growing understanding that the universe was a far bigger place than he'd ever imagined.

How must I have appeared to him? Clothed only in my nightdress, hair long and unbound, eyes wide and alive with understanding.

"Who invited you here?" I asked.

"I came upon my own initiative," said Carruthers.

"You accepted my money to stay away, and yet here you are? An unwelcomed guest at these proceedings."

"I returned to the morgue and the corpse was missing. I had no expectation that you'd misuse the body in such a way. In my line of work, we show reverence to the dead."

"Seth Dawson is clearly not dead," I said. "Focus your eyes on his obvious struggles."

"Something unnatural has occurred," he said.

"You may not be aware, but I'm a doctor. We had only thought Seth dead, but I have worked to heal him."

"That is a lie," he said. "My inspection of the corpse was thorough."

Raw energy moved in the air, a power that I'd not felt in years. Maybe a power I'd never connected with on a truly intimate level.

I breathed it into my lungs. Called it close, and felt it coalesce around me. Hot and writhing against my skin.

"Go now, sir," I said. "You aren't wanted here."

"Wickedness," he said. "Unlike any I've seen."

"You're a fool," I said.

"And you are a witch."

"If you wish me to be."

One simple gesture with my left hand and every candle in the room blazed to life.

Gray rain streaked down the window behind Carruthers, and yellow candlelight revealed the sudden terror in his face. For a moment, he remained locked in place by the weight of my regard. Then his trembling legs carried him quickly from the room, and down the stairs.

"He will return with others," I said.

"Catherine," said Frank. "Are you well?"

Seth continued to scream. His teeth snapped at Frank's hand. The ropes around his chest were growing looser, coming undone.

Seth would soon be free.

"I am perfectly fine, Frank," I said.

I was more than fine. I had never felt so alive. Or perhaps I had, once upon my youth, but so many years had passed, no memories of that time remained.

Louisa had not only restored the missing pieces of my soul; she left some part of herself inside me too. A deep understanding of magick that rearranged every belief I'd had on the subject, revealing the practice's true face with breathtaking clarity. There was no single, right approach to magick. My rituals and correspondences and perfectly arranged symbols would yield results, but they were simply designed to focus my will. Tricks to help me engage with the elemental forces that could make my desires reality. Those forces whispered in my head now, and I felt their presence in the air around me.

Louisa had left me her lifetime of learning, and all the power she'd accessed flowed through me like a noisy river, overflowing its banks. It was too much to reckon in the moment. So, I gave in, let it move through me. Trusted in the universe. I assumed this frenzied sensation would burn off eventually, much like the magick that animated Seth and Frank, but the understanding of how to find it, how to harness it, would remain.

Magick as art, not artifice.

What a gift Louisa had given me.

Chaos continued as those assembled tried to hold Seth still, but I moved through the din, unhurried and untroubled. Whatever sense of loss I felt about Louisa's death, whatever terror and guilt might have consumed me over the surety of Seth's rampage, my newfound wisdom softened it all. Allowed me to think and to act. For certain those emotions would return, and I would deal with them, but in that moment, only the magick mattered.

Aubrey moved aside when I placed a hand on his back, and I stood over Seth as he writhed and screamed, tortured by the magick rebuilding him. His skin was a sickly green, just like Frank, but the rot and corruption that had claimed Frank had not troubled Seth. His eyes were open wide, but they saw nothing. I put a hand on his cheek and one on his chest, felt the sweat and the burning heat of him. Drew on the power I'd accessed to cool him, to calm him, to stall the terror and confusion that drove him to rage. Tears ran down my face. My teeth ground together. Pain rode the connection between us, and I let it come. Seth stilled; his breathing slowed, and his screams quieted. He became again as a man sleeping, and I kept my hands on him to bind him in this state.

"This won't last long," I said. "Rest while you can."

"What did you do?" asked Frank.

"Absorbed some of his discomfort. Made it my own."

"How long until he regains himself?" asked Aubrey.

"I've told you I don't know. When it happens, I'll tell you. Right now, I need you to let me focus on the task at hand."

"That mortician has not been deterred." Thirsty collapsed into a chair by the door, exhausted and no doubt feeling his years. "He strikes me as a born nuisance. He'll be back, and he won't be alone."

"I'll kill him, if need be," said Aubrey.

"There's been enough killing," said Frank.

"My brother's life trumps any number of bodies."

Frank grimaced. "I'm just saying, violence should not be our first choice."

Violence was coming. There was no escaping it. Louisa had revealed the nature of our enemies, and they would never accept us.

"I fear there will be much violence," said Mabel. "Whether we wish it or not."

"You can be certain of it," I said. "Ignorance abides, and bloody conflict is the natural order of things in this place."

"If you can keep him calm," said Frank, "we can walk him out of here and never come back."

"Except we need to rescue Hank," said Mabel.

"What about Hank?" asked Frank.

Mabel remained at the foot of the bed, hands before her in a grasping motion, as if she expected Seth to begin kicking again any second.

"I'm sorry we neglected to tell you," she said. "Hank's been arrested, and they plan to hang him. Dr. Coldbridge and me have plans to break him out, soon as circumstances allow."

"Hold on," said Frank. "Hank is in jail?"

"He is," said Mabel.

"Well, he won't be for long." Frank's features darkened, and his muscles grew taut. He stalked toward the door, abandoning his post at the bed. Thirsty sprang from his seat, put both hands on the bigger man's chest and barred his way.

"One fire at a time, old hoss," said Thirsty.

"We're not leaving him to hang," said Frank.

"Mabel already told you we ain't leaving him. The sheriff come for him yesterday while you were here, put a hurting on a whole bunch of folks at the revue in the process. Don't nobody here plan to let that go without paying them back in spades. But we got some time. We see this resurrection through, then we get Hank out of jail. Right now, we need you right here with us."

Frank shot a scowl my direction, like this whole thing was my fault. Whether it was or not, I was in no place to look backward anymore. To make it out of Fort Worth alive, we'd all have to be looking ahead.

"Hank is fine for now," said Mabel.

"And how do you know that?" asked Frank.

"Dr. Coldbridge talked to him."

"Forgive me if I don't want to take her word for it."

"You'd do well to trust her," said Mabel. "She appears better equipped to weather this storm than the rest of us."

"Save your anger for them that deserve it," said Thirsty. "Right now, we ain't got time for it, and you know that."

Frank withdrew to the window, stared out into the rainy night. So large in that small space that he blocked our view of the outside darkness. His eyes captured the shadows. Every inch of him thrummed with chaotic energy. Whatever magick had driven his killing spree in Montana still lived beneath his skin, and it moved close to the surface of the man. I began to question whether it was entirely under his control now, or if we might have two rampaging creatures on our hands before the sun rose.

"You remember our wedding day?" I asked.

Frank's brows furrowed. He nodded.

"That was a good day, wasn't it?"

"It was, Catherine," he said. "Maybe the best day I ever had."

"We had something, you and me," I said. "It's long gone now, but never forget that we had it. The beautiful days may never outnumber the bad, but they possess more power. They can sustain us if we let them. We are deep in the shadows now, but we're coming out the other side. I promise you that. You are right to question me. I left you there. I ran. But I'm not leaving Hank to his fate. That boy has a curious way of endearing himself to a person. I could not leave him behind, even if I wanted to."

Something loosened in Frank's expression. Tension fled his body, and he leaned back against the windowpane, arms crossed over his chest.

"I don't blame you for running, Catherine," he said.

"You're kind to say it."

"We aren't leaving Hank."

"I promise."

Frank might have grown calmer, but Aubrey still burned with anxiety.

"Tell me what's happening with my brother," he said.

"He is fine, Aubrey. He'll be himself soon enough."

My hands remained on Seth's body, and though his pain was nearly too much to bear, I stayed steady. Felt his heart beating and his lungs pumping as his soul became once again acquainted with its earthly confines.

Most likely I could have kept him that way, until the magick finished its work. Until Seth Dawson rose from the dead, and we all left this place forever.

But then Sheriff Bramlett walked through the door.

And he delivered the gift of violence we'd all been dreading.

The sheriff's pistol was already drawn. His eyes were red, and his hair tangled as a tumbleweed. His nightshirt overhung his pants, and his boots muddied the cedar floorboards. Like me, he'd evidently been summoned from a sound sleep, and appeared out of sorts, but the tableau that greeted him sharpened his focus at once. My trembling hands pressed against the naked man's chest. Aubrey Dawson and Mabel Bones, leaning close over Seth, a brace of pistols belted to both of their bodies, and Mabel clutching her long rifle like Moses with his staff. Thirsty Picket back in his chair, bent over with his thin fingers threaded through his hair. And Frank Humble, the Unkillable Frank Lightning, standing before the window like a storm cloud hiding the face of the moon. Candlelight cast conflicting shadows across the crimson wallpaper. Troublesome spirits capered and danced. All of us stood frozen in the moment, like a sprawling Renaissance painting, the kind I recalled from my travels to Europe as a girl.

Sheriff Bramlett stood there a moment, absorbing every brushstroke of our desperation.

"Here stand the villains!" Jep Carruthers crowded in behind the sheriff, eyes alive with righteous fervor.

Another man joined them. Short in stature, but built like a whiskey barrel. Garbed in black, a clerical collar wrapped so tightly around his throat, it reddened his face. Presumably, the same preacher who'd visited Hank.

"What's happening here?" asked the sheriff.

"Black magic," said Carruthers.

Weary of explaining myself, I opted for silence. Nothing I could say would sway opinions.

"She's a doctor," said Mabel. "This man's wounds were not so severe as many feared."

"His wounds have vanished entirely," said Carruthers.

"Have a care with your guns," said Sheriff Bramlett. "It wouldn't so much as give me heartburn if I had to shoot you dead."

The preacher shoved past Carruthers. He was muscled and primed with youth, and he pushed Thirsty back into his seat when the old cowboy tried to get in his way.

"What ungodly work have you undertaken here?" The preacher's voice was a low rumble, like the movement of a train along a railroad track.

"The doctor saved my brother's life," said Aubrey.

"Back away from him." The preacher attempted to move me aside, but I stood my ground.

"That would be a bad idea," I said.

Carruthers prodded at Seth with one bony finger, like he was testing the firmness of a loaf of bread. "Your place is not to question Preacher Branch, but to follow his word. He is the shepherd here. You are the lamb."

"The shepherd should leave us alone," I said. "Else he might learn his lambs are, in fact, wolves."

"Y'all get over along that wall." Sheriff Bramlett motioned with his pistol, and everyone fell in line beside Frank. I remained standing where I was, trembling from exertion as I worked my magick, trying to keep Seth calm.

"You too, Doctor," said Bramlett.

"You don't understand what's happening here," I said.

"Don't matter, get over there."

"I will not."

"You will." Preacher Branch gave me a shove, sent me toppling onto my knees.

Seth gasped, opened his eyes.

Aubrey helped me to my feet, but Carruthers took up position between Seth and me. Preacher Branch gave Seth's chin a squeeze, turned his head to one side, then the other, like he was inspecting a horse.

Seth snapped at him with his teeth, and the preacher flinched.

"Let me help him," I said.

"If you move," said Bramlett, "I will shoot you in the stomach."

Preacher Branch backed away, put a heavy hand on Carruthers' shoulder and drew him in close. The preacher was young enough to be the mortician's grandson, but he carried himself like he was the oldest and wisest of us all. Black hair fell long and lanky down the sides of his head, and his clean-shaven face was craggy as a mountain range. He appeared a hard man for a preacher, and his manner invited questions about the cleanliness of his character.

Carruthers appeared uncomfortable in the preacher's grip, but made no attempt to squirm away.

"Unbind him," said Preacher Branch. "Then go fetch Dr. Leech. Let him know there is a half-dead man in need of his services. The sheriff and I will deliver these villains to the jail, then I'll return to pray over his soul. If he still lives."

"Yes, sir," said Carruthers.

"Don't untie him," said Frank.

"Close your mouth, creature." Preacher Branch allowed his eyes to wander over Frank's hideous form, and found him wanting.

"If you untie him," said Aubrey, "he will attack you."

"Say he will?" said Carruthers.

"You can be sure of it," said Aubrey.

Preacher Branch pointed at Aubrey. "Sheriff, if this one offers any more sass, populate his body with bullets."

My laughter began as a series of sharp barks, then it rose into a full-throated peal that unnerved everyone in the room, my companions included. Energy sizzled in the air around me. It burned against my skin. Never had I been so delirious with magick. There was so much raw power at play, I couldn't dream of controlling more than a fraction. Suddenly, everything became so clear and so *true* in my mind. Louisa had been right. There was no way to avoid the coming conflict.

This vicious cabal would not be swayed.

We were all of us *oddities*. Dead men walking in the sunlight and women casting spells under cover of the moon.

Unwelcomed strangers, not to be tolerated.

Magick shifted. Expanded. Agitated the shadows.

Candle flames danced and swayed.

There might have been some better course of action. Some way for me to fight back and stop these men. But in that moment, I found I did not want to.

"By all means," I said. "Release the poor soul."

"Catherine!" Frank gaped at me like I'd lost my mind, and it's possible, at least for the moment, that I had.

"Embrace the inevitable," I said. "We might as well try to stop the sun from rising, so certain is the promise of violence."

I laughed again. Felt magick tugging at the loosening threads of my sanity.

"She's a crazy woman," said Carruthers.

"Most of them are," said Preacher Branch.

Carruthers moved with some reluctance, like a powerful sinner on his way to Sunday services. He kept casting wary looks my direction, evidently concerned I was telling the truth. "The man is green. What have they done to him?"

"Step lively," said Preacher Branch.

"Listen to him," I said. "The quicker you let him go, the quicker he can kill every single one of us."

"Her lies taste sweet," said the preacher. "But they provide no nourishment. Do not be deterred."

Carruthers went to work on the ropes, loosening the knots even as Seth began to stir and strain against them.

"The anticipation is the worst part," I said.

"Depends on what you are anticipating," said Preacher Branch. "Looking forward to your death by hanging fills me with delight."

"None of us will live long enough to hang," I said.

Seth started screaming again, and the mortician grew pale as a ghost. When the last rope came loose, Carruthers skittered away like a spider, pressed himself against the wall on the near side of the bed.

"I swear he was dead," said Carruthers.

"Evil is not without power," said Preacher Branch.

Seth sat up in bed, back stiff as lumber. Turned his head to regard the old mortician at his bedside. Even seated, I could tell he was a good six inches taller than before. His skin crawled over the surface of his bones as the magick worked to reanimate him.

"Move away from him!" said Frank.

"Hush, Frank," I said. "He's a harmless lamb."

"Sheriff," said Frank. "We must evacuate this room."

"Don't move away from that wall," said Bramlett.

"I tell you, he is a monster," said Carruthers. "The man is green."

"The doctor shall examine him," said Preacher Branch.

"He smells of rot!" said Carruthers.

"If black magic was the agent of his resurrection," said the preacher, "we shall return him safely to the grave."

"By all means," I said. "Do try."

Seth shifted, slid toward the edge of the bed.

Carruthers appeared ready to back through the wall.

Seth rose to his feet, stiff as a man with an aching back. When his limbs moved, they made a creaky sound like deer hide being stretched for tanning. His screams faded. Became a pleading whine that put me in mind of a mewling cat. Muscles jumped beneath his skin, and his eyes sought out every corner of the room, unable to focus on any one thing for long. I recalled Frank's empty-eyed stare, and understood the terror Seth must be feeling. He lashed out with his arms, grasped at nothing. Tears streaked down his face, and he shook his head violently, as if in denial of his new existence.

"Good lord, I never," said Carruthers.

Seth lunged at the sound of speech. Slammed his fists into Carruthers' chest so hard, the man's ribcage gave way with a sound like a whipcrack.

Carruthers screamed, and Seth lit into him. Pounding the mortician against the wall until the plaster cracked and it appeared the old man might disappear into the wall entirely.

Carruthers' shrieks were wet and desperate.

The sheriff unleashed a barrage of bullets.

And I could barely hear any of it over the sound of my own mad laughter.

Frank climbed over the bed and maneuvered an arm around Seth's throat, hoping to wrestle him into submission.

Several bullets already resided in Seth's torso, but they hadn't slowed him. Sheriff Bramlett fumbled with his gun belt, grasping for more ammunition with unsteady fingers. Thirsty fought to grab Seth's thrashing arm but found himself tossed about like a child's doll. Aubrey rushed in to help, practically climbing his brother's back as the three men fought to subdue him. Mabel Bones drew her pistols, but found no safe targets for her terror. Seth was crawling with bodies, and I imagined it was only instinct that drove her to draw them.

Carruthers was little more than a stain on the wall.

Shadows came to life, emboldened by the chaos. Wild spirits attendant to death and unnatural resurrection. They circled the room in a black rush, like water down a drainpipe. I edged closer, hoping to regain control of Seth, to still his raging soul. But the magick would not be held in sway. There was no mistaking its sentience now. Whatever spirits or gods or elemental forces commanded this power, they had seized control. Might be they'd grant humans like me access to the mysteries, for a time, but now they were wide awake and working toward their own inscrutable ends.

Magick was always on loan. Not something I could ever possess. This understanding came rushing into my mind, another epiphany from Louisa's storehouse of memories and life experiences.

All of this was beyond my control now.

But that didn't mean I could stop trying.

When I tried to close in on the struggle, Preacher Branch knocked me once again to the floor, this time in his haste to escape the melee. He shrieked something about doctors and dead men and unholy hosts, but he was out the door before I could ascertain his motives. No matter. The battle at hand continued in tight quarters. Seth abandoned the late Jep Carruthers in favor of new, more lively opponents. He sloughed off his attackers, easy as doffing a suit coat. Threw them aside and lifted the mattress from the bed. Seth hurled the mattress at Mabel, and she crashed to the ground beneath it, pistols still clutched in her hands.

Frank advanced on Seth again, and the two men grappled for a moment. But Seth was too strong. So invested with killing strength that he initiated a tackle and drove Frank backward.

Frank's feet caught on the mattress, and he stumbled back into the window, shattering the glass. Seth closed in, and shoved Frank the rest of the way through.

Frank made no sound as he fell from the second story, but the impact of his body striking the earth sounded like a cannon shot.

Seth stood before the window. He stared down at Frank. Momentarily transfixed by the cool rain now blowing in from the storm outside. Thirsty helped me lift the mattress away so Mabel could rise, while Aubrey drew both pistols and pointed them at his brother's back. He wore a grim expression, like he'd truly come to understand what a poor decision he'd forced on us all.

Aubrey would never shoot Seth. Not even to save his own skin. Even if he did, those bullets would do little to slow him. Yet he held tight to his guns, like they were the only family he had left.

"Everyone, let's go," I said. "Out of here!"

"Help him!" said Aubrey. "Make him sleep again."

Gunfire sounded. Sheriff Bramlett fired over and over as Seth turned back toward us and began to howl.

We rushed for the door. Seth lifted the oaken bed like it weighed no more than his grandmother's quilt, and hurled it at the sheriff.

Bramlett moved aside in a hurry, but the bed frame clipped him on the shoulder and sent him crashing into the wall. The bed broke apart on impact, leaving all of us more or less entangled in the wooden remains. Bramlett threw aside a splintered bit of the headboard, and crawled through the wreckage. Out the door and onto the second-floor landing. Seth roared forward, knocked aside a chair, and kicked at the skeletal remains of the bed with both feet. Thirsty and I managed to free ourselves. We tumbled through the doorway just as Seth arrived. I reached back for Mabel, grabbed for her hand. But Seth seized Mabel's feet and spun her around, so that she found herself shipwrecked on that raft of broken wood, staring up at the storm cloud preparing to sink her.

Seth grabbed one of the bed legs, arced it backward like he intended to bring it down on her head.

Mabel, faster than lightning, unloaded both her pistols into Seth's face.

Seth staggered backward.

Mabel crawled toward the door, eyes wide with shock, and we pulled her through.

Seth's face was a bloody ruin. He spun in a circle, blinded by the attack, but I could feel the current of power pouring into the room as the magick worked diligently to repair him.

We huddled on the landing that overlooked the saloon floor.

It was not so deep in the night that everyone had cleared out of the Silver Ace, and we found ourselves the target of hard stares and angry shouts. Gunshots and violence were frequent guests of the Silver Ace; that much was evident. The sounds of our struggles enlivened the patrons. Brick, the bartender, had both hands on a shotgun, laid longwise along the bar. Poker players folded their cards. Drunk cowboys rose from their seats. Then I heard Aubrey yelling. Turned to see him framed in the doorway, guns trained on his brother's chest. Aubrey pleaded for Seth to calm down. Reminded him of their siblinghood and the surety of their love for one another. Seth regarded his brother in silence, and I could see bits of his face move, like insects marched beneath the surface. Tiny repairs building one on top of another that would result in the erasure of his injuries.

Peace reigned for a few heartbeats. Aubrey whispered desperate pleas to his brother.

Then Seth regained himself, and with uncanny swiftness, struck Aubrey across the bridge of the nose with the broken bed leg.

Aubrey went down, and did not rise.

"Everyone, get out of here!" I yelled over the banister at the assembled patrons, even as I moved to help Mabel down the stairs. Thirsty was right behind us. Sheriff Bramlett had descended in a hurry, and joined those onlookers staring up at the landing as Seth Dawson crashed through the doorway and stood beside the railing, surveying the dozen or so assembled souls like an angry god, looking down from the heavens.

Thirsty lagged behind, and when we reached the ground floor, I saw he'd crept back up the stairs.

"Don't come no closer, monster!" Bramlett shouted up at Seth, pistols aimed at him. Loud and seemingly in charge now that he'd managed to distance himself somewhat from the danger.

Seth grunted, turned toward the stairs. Thirsty sidestepped in a hurry, whooped like a wild man, and gave Seth a rough shove that sent him off balance and toppling over the railing.

Seth fell like a boulder, crashed into a table, and reduced it to splinters.

A pair of lanky cowboys approached, likely comfortable in their belief that no person would rise from such a fall. But that notion vanished when Seth got to his knees, pulled one of the cowboys to the ground, and drove his head against the floor. The other cowboy rushed in, thinking to wrestle Seth away, but the dead man put an arm around his throat and squeezed until the sound of snapping bones drew gasps and sudden action from everyone else in the room.

Guns were discouraged in the Silver Ace, but in this part of town, such restrictions were not strictly enforced. Everyone in the room produced pistols, and Brick rounded the bar with his shotgun at his hip, ready for action.

"Sit yourself on the ground," said Brick.

Seth let the broken cowboy fall to the floor. Rose to his feet and proceeded directly toward Brick.

No telling how many guns fired then. Ten, maybe twelve shots. And in such close quarters, nearly every one of them a clean hit. But, of course, Seth was not slowed. He slapped at his bullet holes with giant palms, like they were no more irritating than bee stings. Saw the first cowboy who'd approached him lying still on the ground, and commenced to stomp on his head.

"Lord, he'll kill them all." Thirsty had trotted down the stairs with more speed than I would have credited him, and he stood with Mabel and me, absorbing the fear and the fatalism that ran roughshod through the saloon.

Brick drew in close and pulled the shotgun trigger.

Seth doubled over, and fell to his knees again.

"That put him down quick," said one of the patrons, a grinning man in a fancy blue suit with a tight grip on his playing cards, like the game might resume just as soon as this minor unpleasantness was dispatched.

Brick shook with anger. "I hate to do it. But you come in my place and behave in such a fashion, you get what you get."

"Move away!" I said. "He won't stay down for long."

"Everyone clear out of here!" said Sheriff Bramlett.

"He's not likely to trouble us further," said Brick.

Seth worked slowly back to a standing position. Blood poured in a rush from his midsection, like someone had overturned a slaughterhouse bucket.

"What in creation?" said Brick.

"He's a demon," said Bramlett.

"He's what, now?"

"Summoned by a witch." Sheriff Bramlett pointed my direction when he spoke, but all eyes remained on Seth, who had both hands covering the hole in his stomach.

Frank banged in through the swinging doors behind us, soaked by the rain but otherwise no worse for the wear. Presumably if his body still healed from arrow strikes and bullet wounds, a two-story fall was a minor chore. A few eyes sought Frank out, recognized him as the Unkillable Frank Lightning. And I could practically read their minds as they considered Frank's nature, and compared it to that of the gut-shot man rising again to his full height, wounds repairing before their eyes. The unnatural green skin. The uncanny healing ability. Twin giants with the talent to strike fear and awe. Everyone's terror ran hot. Self-preservation became the coin of the realm. And if they managed to subdue Seth somehow, I had no doubt they'd turn their attention to the rest of us.

"Frank, we need to get him out of here," I said.

Seth eyed Brick, and the bartender's brow furrowed. He still had his shotgun at the ready, but seemed confused that he might have to pull the trigger again.

Seth opened his mouth, but no sound came out.

Then he moved with that unnatural speed, bowled into Brick, and knocked him back against the bar. Brick tried to fire again but Seth swatted the gun aside and the blast struck the blue-suited man in the chest. He dropped with rapid finality. His fistful of cards drifted down and settled upon his bloody corpse.

Every gun in the room went off then, none with any qualms about striking poor Brick, who was engaged in a one-sided wrestling match with Seth.

"Thirsty, go get us some horses," said Frank. "And ropes. We need to lure him out of here. If we can get him outside, maybe we can get him tied up. Drag him away from all this. I don't know. But we need to remove him from town before he kills everyone here."

Seth was already well on his way to killing Brick, and everyone else seemed lined up to follow.

"I'll be fleet of foot." Thirsty left the saloon in search of horses, just as Seth found his voice again and unleashed a chilling scream.

Several people closed in, tried to climb on Seth, but he proceeded to bash Brick against the bar again and again. The man was plainly dead, but Seth remained diligent, possessed as he was by supernatural strength, and cursed with a killer's mind. Sheriff Bramlett kept at a safe remove, but he circled around the room, drawing closer to the bar. Lightning flashed outside, and thunder followed close on its heels, but the cold rain grew silent. Sweat poured down my neck. The room was sticky, hot with magick. Breaking bones and gunshots and terrified screams assaulted my ears, and I felt a faintness begin to weigh me down, like all the guilt and anger I'd felt for half my lifetime was returning in a rush. Then Frank put a steadying hand on my shoulder. Spoke in a low, even voice, that cut through the chaos and set me back on the path.

"You need to get Hank," he said.

"Okay." I nodded, still half in a daze.

"I'll stay here," he said. "Try to help? I don't know. At the very least, I'll try to contain the violence until we can lure Seth away. Take Mabel and break Hank out. Get him to Cowboy Dan or anyone else at the Wild West Revue, and they'll see he's taken to safety. Can you do that, Catherine?"

"I told you I would," I said.

"I'll meet you . . . somewhere," he said.

"Mabel, have you reloaded your guns?" I asked.

"Yes, ma'am," she said.

"And you are willing to accompany me on a jailbreak?"

"I would very much enjoy it."

Seth was a whirling dervish in the middle of the bar, battling attackers on all sides. Blood colored the floor and bent bodies lay strewn at unnatural angles near Seth's feet. Whimpers and cries and shrieks abounded. Sheriff Bramlett closed in, a pistol in one hand, and one of the saloon's oil lanterns in the other, holding it high over his head like an explorer, descending into a bottomless cavern. Mabel and I were ready to go, but the mad fire in Bramlett's expression caught hold and held me.

"I'll burn you back to Hell, you damned old son of a bitch!" Bramlett hefted the lantern and hurled it at Seth.

His aim was true. The lantern hit Seth square in the face. His head caught fire. Lantern oil coursed down his body, blazing a trail for the flames to follow.

Seth had a young cowboy in a bear hug, and that man caught
fire too. Seth continued to spin, dragging the burning man in circles. Smoke started to choke the room, and the stench was foul.

Everyone backed up in a hurry, but those who'd been pressing
the attack were too close to flee. Seth continued fighting, as if
the flames were nothing more than a fine new set of clothes. He
reached out with burning arms, enveloped screaming men in the
growing fire. Angry flames chased along the liquor-slicked bar
top, and made hungry advances against the tablecloths. Electric
lights fluttered, and oil lanterns popped and exploded around
the room as the fire took hold. It consumed overturned chairs
and blackened the cedar floorboards. Bramlett ran from the inferno, eyes wild, and screaming about righteous fire. He angled
for the door, nearly knocked Mabel over as he fled into the night.

"You need to go, now!" said Frank.

"This whole place will burn down," I said.

"Get Hank! I'll tend to this. Go!"

And so, I left the Silver Ace for the last time, Mabel hot on my
heels.

Frank Humble remained inside, to face the fire alone.

Bullets and Broken Bodies

From the Jail to the Fairgrounds, Fort Worth, Texas
Spring 1905

THE CLOUDS WERE GONE, leaving a tangled nest of stars visible in the night sky. Magick moved through the streets of Fort Worth, and the constellations writhed in the heavens, dancing to their for-ever song. A cannonade of thunder continued in the distance. The air was thick and smelled like wet cattle. Still outfitted in only my nightdress, I ran up the street, concentrating on the feel of my bare feet against the muddy earth. Some of the Fort Worth roads were paved with ochre bricks, but this part of town was still a riot of mud and wagon ruts, and I felt the ground pulling me closer to myself, even as the magick threatened to lift me up and carry me away forever.

Carousers and night people haunted the shadows and congre-gated in the alleyways; every eye seemed to follow as we hurried toward the jail. I spotted Preacher Branch amid a conspiratorial circle of men on the porch of a shuttered mercantile building, no doubt inciting them to join his cause, but there was no time to investigate. Our welcome in Fort Worth had expired, and leav-ing with the greatest possible haste was our only hope of evading the noose.

Mabel hurried along at my side, checking to make sure her pistols were fully loaded. Eyes on the move. Her costume bonnet had fallen off in the struggle, and her hair had come undone so that it flowed in her wake like a golden river.

"How many deputies were there before?" she asked.

"Three, I think," I said.

"I'd prefer not to kill anyone."

"That is not my plan," I said.

"Have you a plan then?"

"Mabel, we don't have the luxury of time. We can't deliberate over every detail. Just walk in there with your guns out and hope for the best."

And that's precisely what we did.

As we entered the jail, I recalled the fleeing Sheriff Bramlett, and wondered if he might have returned to fetch some help, but there were only two deputies there to greet us, and neither expected the arrival of a half-dressed woman with a windstorm of graying hair, or a hard-eyed beauty with twin pistols drawn and held out before her at arm's length. There was no mistaking the look in Mabel's eyes. No questioning our resolve. And so, when Mabel demanded they drop their gun belts on the ground and take us back to the cells, the deputies complied with a few sharp comments but no real resistance.

Hank was standing with his hands grasping the iron bars when we arrived, and without delay, we released the boy from his cell, and left the two deputies in his place.

"I wasn't expecting y'all so soon," he said.

"External forces have accelerated our departure," I said.

We returned to the office, and I fished through the ring of keys that Mabel had demanded from the deputies. Among the cell keys and the front door key was a small, brass model that fit the glass cabinet housing the sheriff's collection of firearms. I unlocked the door, and Hank regarded the arsenal with an expression usually reserved for religious zealots. Hank dug in like a starving man at a fine dinner table, eventually settled on a burnished leather gun belt studded with conchos that housed a heavy revolver. The gun shone like the sun in the swaying lantern light.

"A Peacemaker," he said. "This'll do."

"Sure that's your size?" I asked.

"Used to have one just like it."

"Okay, then."

Hank loaded the gun belt with shells, then filled his pockets. "What do you want? Maybe a shotgun?"

"I'll trust the guns to the two of you."

"You will proceed unarmed?" he said.

"As I always have. I have neither the time nor desire to embrace the way of the gun."

Hank shook his head, confused perhaps as to why I'd not want a gun in the middle of a jailbreak. But I was beyond killing someone. Beyond even defending myself. I only wanted to get the boy out of town, and all the other endangered souls with him.

Laughter erupted outside.

Maybe drunks, maybe ghosts. Who could say?

Mabel holstered her pistols, sought out a long rifle from the cabinet. "I left my Winchester back in Seth's room, and I doubt I'll be given leave to retrieve it. This one's a good match, though."

"We musn't linger," I said.

"Where we going?" asked Hank.

"To Cowboy Dan," I said. "Frank says he'll be willing to spirit you away from here."

Magick itched at my brain and stoked my nerves. Terror over

what must still be transpiring at the Silver Ace worked against my forward motion.

But we had to walk back out into the night.

There was no other choice.

"Let's go then." Mabel opened the door, peered out into the street. A gun fired. Mabel stumbled back, fell into my arms.

Sheriff Bramlett stepped into the doorway. Smoking pistol at his hip. He was sweaty and heaving, like he'd been running for his life. His body shook, and fear pulled at the edges of his eyes. Earlier in the day, he'd been unpleasant, but in command of his faculties. In the interim, he'd become wild. One shoulder hung lower than the other, perhaps injured when Seth hit him with the bed. Bramlett's teeth were stained with blood, and he smelled like he'd lost control of his bladder. Bramlett might have been possessed by simple terror, or by one of the roaming spirits of this place. Either way, he'd been reshaped into a frightened animal.

"I won't allow you to escape," he said.

"We don't want to *escape*," I said. "We just want to *leave*."

"Doesn't matter. We'll bury you here."

"Let us go, and you won't see our faces again."

"Cover those faces in grave dirt, and it's the same outcome."

"We didn't harm your deputies." Mabel's voice was strong and insistent. Blood stained her dress, seeped from a wound in her shoulder, but she retained her defiance.

Bramlett looked around the room, as if just realizing his deputies were not at their post. He hissed through his teeth when his eyes settled on Hank, but he kept the gun pointed right at Mabel. Right at me. Hank was fast, but I imagine he knew better than to try to draw on the sheriff, with the man's finger trembling against the trigger. Mabel steadied herself, stared back at Bramlett as if challenging him to shoot her again. Bramlett seemed consumed by the moment, absorbed in the dark reality of the blood and fire that chased us all; some small part of him hinged upon the point between justice and violence, waiting for the universe to give him a sign.

I wished for a spell. Something to calm him.

Louisa's voice came in a whisper, words spoken only for me. The barrier between life and death had grown thinner than ever, and I could almost feel her lips against my ears as they revealed everything I needed to hear.

I began to chant. Joined my voice to Louisa's and we spoke our will together.

Bramlett tensed up at once.

"Hush yourself!" he said.

There was nothing for it but to proceed. My lips moved, but my words became silent. For it did not matter if these words were spoken aloud, or only in my heart, they drew from the same well of power. A great weariness evinced itself in Bramlett's manner; his eyelids began to sag, and he became more stooped, like the world had settled heavily upon his back. But he remained steady with his pistol. The sheriff spoke some manner of threat or plea, but the sound of his voice could not overcome the noise in my head, and I proceeded with my chant, even as he moved so close that the barrel of his pistol rested against Mabel's midsection. Then his grip began to waver. His face flushed red, and tears welled in his eyes.

I moved Mabel aside and stood before Bramlett, let my hand fall on his forearm and gently guided his pistol arm downward until the weapon pointed at the floor.

Then I put my cold hands on his cheeks, and placed my forehead against his. "We will not harm you, but we have to leave."

Bramlett nodded, tears running down his face.

"Would you mind terribly, surrendering your gun?"

He nodded again, handed me the pistol.

Regret touched his heart, revealed itself in his features, a creeping revelation. It moved slow, like the moon as it travels across the face of the sun. Then it settled inside his bones, and the man was *done*. Bramlett would recover himself soon enough, but for now he was left enthralled by the reflected image of his every misdeed. Made to stare into the mirror of his existence and face down every wrong for which he deserved blame.

I can't imagine the horror I'd feel if someone turned that same mirror toward me.

"Hank?" I said.

"Ma'am?"

"This enchantment is likely to be short-lived, so please escort the sheriff to the cells without delay."

Hank approached, got a grip on Bramlett's arm, and the sheriff followed meekly along as Hank led him toward the cells.

"Don't mistreat him, Hank." I said.

"I am not that sort of person," said Hank.

"I know, Hank. And thank you."

I began to examine Mabel's wounds. Thankfully, the bullet had passed clean through and avoided any critical bones or organs. Blood seeped from a wound on the front of her left shoulder, and ran faster from the place on her upper back where the bullet made its exit. But this was no fatal shot. So long as the wound was well tended, Mabel would recover fully. I cast about the room for some sort of cloth, settled on a couple of cotton shirts hanging on a coatrack. If not entirely clean, they at least smelled laundered, and I used them to bind Mabel's wounds, to slow the flow of blood. Mabel did not so much as flinch as I worked at her injuries.

"You are taking this in stride."

"I have not always been the refined lady I am now," Mabel said with a grin. "I was a true reprobate in my youth. I'm no stranger to jails."

"You don't strike me as a villain."

"Not a villain, but at the very least a criminal."

"I find that hard to credit," I said.

"My attempted notoriety was half-hearted. I'll admit that much. Rode with some fellows called themselves the Elder Gang. Talked big about being bank robbers, and might be they held up one or two before I joined them. On one occasion, I did help rob a mercantile. But mostly we loitered in saloons and endeavored to look mean. We cheated at poker, a time or two. Intimidated barkeeps for free drinks and chuck steaks. Please don't let my past color your opinion of me, Dr. Coldbridge. My parents orphaned me young, and being adrift in the world with scoundrels is often better than enduring it alone."

"No one has less right to judge you than me."

"I am a good person, most days," she said.

"That, I believe."

"You are too," she said. "You'll figure that out."

"Now we have returned to the realm of fiction."

"Listen here. If I die, please do not feel obligated to bring me back to life. I'd as soon be at rest."

"You aren't going to die, Mabel. And my resurrecting days are done."

"Ma'am, if you don't mind me saying, I believe that's for the best."

When I finished, Mabel's arm hung in a makeshift sling, and though red with blood, the shirts seemed to have slowed the flow.

"Once we pass these trials, I can provide better care. But I cannot affect an immediate change in your condition, even with magick. We must move quickly."

"I won't slow us." Mabel was pale and slick with sweat, but she was steady on her feet, and refused to show the pain she must be feeling.

Hank returned and tossed the ring of keys on the sheriff's desk. He was less skilled at hiding his distress than Mabel, and he fretted over the young woman like she was a child, and he was her parent.

"Can't believe you got shot on my account," he said.

"I don't blame you for it."

"Well, I do. You sure that bandage will suffice?"

"Dr. Coldbridge knows her business," said Mabel.

"You can call me Catherine," I said.

"Yes, ma'am," said Mabel.

"Hank, you locked him up?" I asked.

"Yes, I did, and with delight. One of them fiends spit in my food, I'm pretty sure."

"Okay, then. Let's go. We walk out like we've done nothing wrong. And we don't stop walking until we reach the fairgrounds."

"Where do we go from there?" asked Hank.

"As far away from Fort Worth as we can get."

The Silver Ace was an inferno. Fire chased along every wall and flowed upward from the second-story windows like hellish rivers, spilling into the sky. Half of the awning had fallen onto the raised porch, causing it to collapse, and the flames made hungry advances on the buildings standing to either side of the doomed saloon. A bucket brigade was already at work by the time we reached the scene, but each pail of water they sloshed against the fire made it more evident that the place was beyond saving. I will admit some shame that my first concern was for my leather book and other belongings, surely consumed by now, but then I noticed the pair of burning men, trading blows in the middle of the street, and all thought of anything else vanished.

Seth Dawson had grown a foot and a half since his resurrection; every inch of him was ablaze, and he thrashed about like an angry giant, arms flailing and feet stomping, a creature of rage and pain. Frank stood tall before Seth. One of his arms was on fire and the rest of him was sure to follow. Dodging Seth's grasping hands, and trying to lure him farther from the men trying to save the Silver Ace, farther from anyone he might hurt. Thirsty Picket sat astride a white mare, lasso hanging limp in his hands like he was unsure what he was supposed to do with it. He led a couple of other horses on a line behind him, but it seemed he'd arrived too late to be of much use in luring Seth away.

"Frank!" Hank sprinted past me, boots digging into the mud. His new Peacemaker pistol flowed like mercury from his holster into his hand, and he fired so fast and true, the booming sound of the gun was in my ears before I realized what he was doing.

Seth staggered, but was not deterred.

"Stay back, kid!" Frank held a hand out toward Hank, froze the boy in his tracks. Frank scampered up the road, away from us all, his back trailing flames. Seth lumbered after him, silent as the grave, black smoke churning in his wake like he was a smokestack.

Thirsty moved the horses, circled behind Seth like he was trying to herd a steer.

Mabel and I caught up with Hank, and I put my arms around him, hugging him from behind. Afraid he'd leap into the fray to save Frank.

"Frank has a plan," I said. "He talked about it."

"He's on fire!" said Hank.

Never had I felt the sheer weight of magick moving in the air as I did that night. Unseen forces laboring to undo all the damage done to Seth's body. And to Frank's. The way the fire swayed and danced, I could no longer tell the spirits from the shadows, but I could sense those mysterious beings riding the heat currents, and striving to fulfill their inscrutable purpose. But fire was its own elemental force. It would not be forestalled for long. And as Seth moved up the street, he began to slow and stumble. Frank stripped away his burning shirt, fell to the ground and rolled on his back, trying to put out the fire chewing at his green skin. Frank kept eyes on Seth, but Seth took three more steps toward him before falling to his knees.

Even magick could not animate him forever.

We hurried to help Frank, but he'd already managed to douse the flames from his body.

Seth remained on his knees a moment, then fell to his back, still burning like a campfire in the middle of the street. Shouted commands and terrified cries echoed in the night as the people of Fort Worth assembled. The violent rainstorms that had plagued the region since my arrival were now sorely missed, but they seemed reluctant to return. Even the clouds had fled, and the fat white moon gazed down on the proceedings with concern. Somewhere, a church bell rang out an alarm. People gathered as Seth burned, many of them carrying lanterns or torches, even though the burning corpse of the Silver Ace lit up this part of the city like high noon.

Frank rose to his feet. Leaned against Hank while he regained his strength. "Seth is still alive. We can't leave him like this."

And he was right. Seth was motionless, but the magick kept the blood moving inside what remained of him.

A man emerged from the crowd, toting a large metal bucket, and dumped it over Seth's body with a crackle and a hiss. He shook the bucket, taking care to distribute the water so that every flame was extinguished. The man knelt beside Seth, reached for his hand then thought better of it. He looked up at us, and I realized it was Aubrey, his handsome face bloody and smashed almost beyond recognition from the attack with the bed leg. He was now a closer match for his brother than he'd ever been before.

"Please get us away from here." Aubrey spoke through a mouthful of shattered teeth, and his voice came out small and plaintive.

"We will, Aubrey."

"Best we move fast," said Mabel.

People continued to pour into the street, half of them fighting the fire, the rest reaching the conclusion that the assembled band of strangers was surely to blame for all this chaos.

Frank waved over to Thirsty. "Let's go."

Thirsty nodded, threw the lasso end of his rope down toward us. "We cannot be delicate in our maneuvering. Get that around his shoulders and we'll ride."

"You can't drag him!" said Aubrey.

"That's exactly what I mean to do," said Thirsty. "Unless you can manage to get him in the saddle on one of these horses."

"You'll take the hide off his back," said Aubrey.

"Ain't no hide left now," said Thirsty. "And he'll be worse off still if we leave him to these people."

The Aubrey I'd met in St. Louis would surely have put up more of a fight, but our short time in Texas had broken us all in some way. He watched meekly as Frank bound the rope around Seth and knotted it tight. All around us, people came alive with anger, figuring out our plan was to flee. Hank and Mabel discouraged any bold actors with their brandished weapons, and the locals were content for now to haunt us from a distance, but their eyes promised retribution.

"Time to leave," said Frank.

At Frank's urging, Mabel and Hank saddled the two horses on Thirsty's line. They looked young and tired and forlorn in the fire-lit darkness. The horses stamped and shifted as their riders settled in. Then Thirsty gave a sharp whistle, and his mare lurched forward. The rope around Seth yanked him into motion, and soon all three horses were at a slow trot, Seth's blackened form dragging along behind. The crowd gasped. They moved forward as a mass, but when Frank waved his arms and shouted at them to keep away, they complied. Frank was forever an intimidating sight. Aubrey drew his pistol, summoned the remnants of his resolve. Together they were enough to slow the crowd, but somewhere at the fringes of night I could hear Preacher Branch's voice, shouting about demons and witches, and I knew we'd better be gone before his words frightened everyone into motion again.

"God damn preacher," said Aubrey.

"Aubrey, come along."

I steered Aubrey away from the crowd and we followed the path of the departing horses. They'd already disappeared beyond the halo of firelight, giving the eerie sensation that night had swallowed them whole.

Frank walked beside us with a limp, and I realized the fire had removed much of the skin from his left leg, in addition to the charred black places on his back and arms. He gritted his teeth and urged us to hurry. Coughed and gagged and spat up blood.

The crowd regarded our departure with hostility.

They shouted insults and shook their torches.

But they did not follow. They were afraid. Soon enough, though, they'd shame one another into hunting us down.

We had to make sure we were already gone.

We reached the field near the train station where the Wild West Revue situated their operation, and Cowboy Dan himself met us there to escort us through the maze of wind-tossed tents and muddy animal pens. Night flowed black as ink through the outskirts of Fort Worth, and I stayed close behind the old raconteur, for fear he'd disappear into the darkness and leave us lost there forever. Thirsty and the others on horseback had preceded our arrival by a good ten minutes, and Cowboy Dan assured us plans for our escape from the city were already in motion.

"They told me you'd be along," he said.

"We appreciate you taking us in," I said.

"You are friends of Frank. And besides, I would not leave you to the untender mercies of the weak-minded and the wicked."

Cowboy Dan looked like a different man. He wore plain denim pants and a faded cotton shirt, a far cry from the finery of his performance outfit. His boots were tall and black, caked with mud. He wore no hat, and though his white hair fell long down his neck, his scalp was bald and wrinkled. Those same wrinkles pulled at his eyes, and his furrowed cheeks sank inward when he grinned, causing him to look older, perhaps, than he really was. But there was a real fire in his expression. One that coaxed confidence when none should exist. Mischief burned in that old man, and the conspiratorial way he embraced us caused me to question the uncharitable view I'd formed of him. Cowboy Dan possessed an authenticity that I hadn't reckoned. Perhaps more of his tall tales hewed closer to the truth than I'd imagined.

"I'm sorry for the trouble I brought," I said.

"Hardly the first bit of strife I've seen," he said.

"Dan has a thick hide," said Frank. "He collects trouble like a miser collects gold coins."

Dan cackled. "Life must be seasoned with danger, else there's no real taste to it. So my old mother used to say, and she was a wild one indeed. Don't fret over any of this, Dr. Coldbridge. We've endured our share of ire from the locals over the years. Most cities embrace our arrival as something to be celebrated, but there are some mirthless few who are eager to provide us an early escort from the premises. We received quite a welcome here, and I think folks thoroughly enjoyed our presentation. They aren't to blame for the low rascals who tossed my camp and harmed my performers. Those people, I wish to thwart. Assisting your escape from them will lighten my heart. You seem to be our kind of people. Strange and wonderful. Do not forget that about yourself. And do not let men with selfish morals cause you to question your own mind."

A lump rose in my throat. I had not expected such kindness from Cowboy Dan, nor such insight. Our current troubles were all on my ledger, no matter what he might say. But I appreciated his attempt to relieve my blame.

"I'm sorry I have to go too," said Frank.

Cowboy Dan waved him off. "We'll miss you, but the show will continue. The Wild West Revue was turning heads long before the Unkillable Frank Lightning joined the bill. We shall regroup. Word is, there's a fellow down in Austin can turn himself into a coyote. I don't know if there's truth to the stories, but he'd make a mighty fine addition to the show."

"I'd pay to see that," said Aubrey.

"See, there you go!" said Dan. "Here now, we've arrived. Climb on up into the wagon and get moving."

Before us was Dan's rickety old stagecoach, the *Golden Gulch*. Like Dan himself, the coach appeared far more world-weary up close, though a recent coat of blue paint hid the worst of the splintering. The coach angled slightly to one side, likely the victim of too many raucous performances. Seth Dawson's charred body lay strapped to the top, where a porter might otherwise stash the luggage. I could not tell whether he still drew breath, but at the very least he was quite still and posed no immediate threat. Thirsty perched up on the driver's box, and he slapped his palm against the seat beside him, an invitation to ride.

"Hustle up here, Frank," he said. "Time's wasting."

Frank turned to Cowboy Dan. "You're giving us the stage? We can't take this."

"Boy, that is the twelfth *Golden Gulch* stage I've owned since starting the show. The genuine article is overturned in a snake-haunted draw somewhere in the territories. I'll have no trouble finding a suitable replacement. Old relics like this are common as arrowheads in the sand around here."

The stagecoach door swung open, and Mabel peeked out, her hair in tangles and her eyes bright with hope. The lantern hanging from the side of the coach colored her pale face yellow and illuminated the vehicle's dank interior. The stench of mold and rotting wood wafted from inside, and the red velvet seat cushions appeared stained and torn, but the prospect of escape made the whole affair seem grand as a New York City hotel. Hank climbed in and sat beside Mabel. Aubrey and I followed, and took the seat opposite them, so that we faced the back of the coach. The vehicle shuddered as Frank ascended to the driver's box and took the seat beside Thirsty. The team of horses bound to the coach whinnied and clapped their shod feet against the earth, eager for motion.

I recalled with eerie clarity the last time the two of them drove the coach.

The roaring crowd and the flurry of arrows.

Both men overrun by a fictional assault.

Now the gunfire and the anger were real. But as I sat there listening to Cowboy Dan giving directions to Thirsty and Frank, the joviality in his voice gave me comfort. Made me optimistic that every single one of us would escape this place and live to see morning.

It was a fool's hope.

"I will miss you, young Hank." Dan leaned into the coach and slapped the boy on the knee.

"Well, I hate I have to go."

"No other choice," said Dan. "Though if you seek me out somewhere down the road, I shall always have a home for you. But I believe there are better things in store for the Hurricane Kid than growing old in a travelling revue. Explore the world and conquer it."

Hank's lip trembled, and he turned his face to the shadows. I recalled the stories he'd shared of his life, and the family he'd lost. There was no mistaking the fear he felt at the prospect of rebuilding that life yet again.

"Thank you for taking me in." Mabel's eyes were wet with tears as she reached over and shook Dan's hand. "There are some who'd have not been so charitable."

"Remember," said Dan, "the world is not so terrible a place, though some seek to make it so. Avoid that sort of rascal, and you shall go far."

"Avoiding them is the hard part."

"Indeed, it is," said Dan.

"I'll miss the revue."

"Mabel, you'll always have a home here too. You are the finest trick shot I ever saw."

"Hey!" Hank wiped his nose on his sleeve, and narrowed his eyes in mild disgust.

"Rest easy, boy. She's a few years older. With time and practice, you might become her equal."

Thirsty hollered down from the driver's box. "We stay here much longer, and we'll be staying here for good."

"Thank you for everything," I said.

Cowboy Dan reached like he was going to tip his hat to me, then realized he wasn't wearing it. His fingers threaded back through his hair, and he favored me with a toothy smile. "Take care of these good people."

Then he closed the stagecoach door, and slapped the side panel to signal Thirsty. The old cowboy wasted not a second, putting the team into motion with a snap of the reins.

Inside the coach, the four of us sat silent and exhausted, and I was seized by the unhappy notion that we'd all been sealed inside the same rolling tomb. Pale faces floated in the darkness, peering at one another as if seeking solace or certainty that we'd overcome our trials, but no such comfort was offered. The people of the Wild West Revue peered at us through the windows as we moved through the rows of tents, picking up speed. Memories of gunfire echoed in this place. Cheers and laughter and shrieks of joy remained behind; ghosts of good times not long gone. But we were awash in violence now. More visceral and final than anything staged by Cowboy Dan and his performers.

The stagecoach fled the city with all possible swiftness, and it wasn't long before black night swallowed us whole.

The Last Ride of the *Golden Gulch*
From Fort Worth into the Wild Heart of Texas
Spring 1905

OUR ENEMIES' APPROACH began as a pinprick of light over the vastness of the prairie.

The stagecoach shuddered over the uneven terrain; the motion rattled our bones, and bounced us against the poorly cushioned seats. But sleep campaigned against all discomfort. I surrendered to my exhaustion, let it carry me to a place of stillness and dreamy peace. For the first time in forever, I was following a path chosen for me, instead of blazing one for myself. Frank and Thirsty had set a course, and I would trust their abilities to get us there. Freedom from action was a notion that brought me no small measure of relief, and I would have gladly slept away my lifetime in that rickety coach as it carried us across the endless plains, but of course, such dreams can only be imagined, never lived. Such escapes from the sharp perils of life can only be temporary.

Reality is cold and unforgiving.

Frank hammered on the side of the stagecoach, yanked me from my slumber with a violent start.

"We are pursued!" he yelled.

I pushed aside the moth-chewed curtain from the window, and stuck my head out to look behind us. And I saw them as an orange glow, distant but growing larger. Men on horseback, most like. Carrying lanterns or torches. Outpacing us would be a simple matter. Mabel looked out the opposite window, drew her head back inside hurriedly. She appeared sweaty and sick, and the shirts binding her shoulder in a sling were soaked through with blood, but she looked to the preparation of the pistols belted over her dress, and made certain her rifle was loaded as well. A symphony of metal sounded out as my other companions followed her lead.

"Trade places with me," said Mabel.

"What will it matter?" I asked.

"You are no marksman. I'd like to slow a few of them down before they're on top of us."

It was clumsy work in the close quarters, but Mabel managed to climb over into my seat, and I fell back into hers with a fresh ache in my back. From her new vantage, Mabel leaned out the window with her rifle, peered out behind us, and set her sights upon the approaching riders.

Mabel pulled herself back inside. "Not close enough yet. But they're coming real soon."

Hank had his Peacemaker in his lap, both hands placed serenely overtop it, prepared for the inevitability of its barking report. He was cool as any young man seated in the front church pew. Quiet, as if contemplating his mortality. I recalled the iron nail in his shirt pocket, and hoped his mother's magick would be enough to carry him through another violent scrape. Aubrey had both of his pistols crossed over his chest, and he must have found some of his old spirit, for he seemed suddenly alive with vigor, as if prepared to leap from the coach and face down our pursuers alone. His smile had returned too. Marred by blood and broken bone, but every bit as self-assured.

"I'd rather fight than run, anyway," he said.

"I'd rather we all live," I said.

"That seems unlikely at this juncture," he said. "But we can surely levy a toll of blood before we join the endless night."

"Your nihilism is premature," I said. "We don't know how many riders are following."

"Enough," he said. "You can be sure of it."

And I knew he was right. Whether they'd rampaged through the Wild West Revue on their way out of town, or steered around the fairgrounds, someone had followed. Someone had spied us leaving. The smallness of our band was known, and our isolation assured no escape. It would not take many attackers to overpower us, and there was no question this unjust posse rode with confidence in their numbers.

"I don't wish to kill anyone," said Hank.

"Wishes are worthless," said Aubrey. "Ready your gun."

"It's ready enough."

"Killing is easy as moving your finger. You won't hesitate. You did not stay your hand against my brother, did you?"

"I suppose not."

"Soon, you'll be a practiced killer."

"Silence is your friend, Aubrey," I said. "Every time you speak it highlights the deficiencies in your character."

"You'll not have to endure me for much longer."

"Well, that's a blessing."

"They're drawing closer." Mabel peeked out the window again. "Oh, there's a lot of them. More than a dozen, I'd say."

Gunshots echoed in the distance.

Our stagecoach accelerated. Horse hooves pounded against

the hard earth. But our pursuers gained ground. Gunfire intensified. And then they were close enough we could hear the hoofbeats of their horses, joining our own.

"Let the killing commence." Aubrey held his pistol out the window and fired blindly at the retreating darkness, his smile teetering on madness.

Mabel took a more measured approach. She leaned out with her rifle, took careful aim, and fired.

"A clean hit," she said. "I saw the man fall."

"I'm the one shot him," said Aubrey.

"Your wild aim caused them no trouble." Mabel leaned out again, repeated her firing motion, and dropped another rider easy as a Sunday nap.

"Have you discouraged them?" I asked.

"No, they appear to be a stubborn bunch."

And they were. Within moments, they'd drawn even with the hurtling stagecoach, and enveloped us. Torchlight streaked past and black horses broke into view like pieces of night, detached from the horizon. Aubrey cut loose with both pistols, dropping the nearest rider with an anguished scream and a spray of blood. But the men returned fire. Bullets whistled through the coach, thudded into the wood near Mabel's head. Splinters flew and the coach door began to rattle on its hinges. Despite his protest, Hank's survival instinct activated, and he fired out the window as well. I cannot say if he struck anyone, but he emptied his gun in a hurry, and reloaded as fast as possible with trembling fingers. The riders having surrounded us, Mabel abandoned her rifle, and brought her pistols to bear on the opposite side of the coach, dealing damage with every bullet, and causing the riders to drop back out of her line of fire.

My mind called out desperately to the universe, but there was no answer. Not that I expected one. Magick is not a blunt instrument. Not a tool to sweep all the opposing game pieces off the board. Magick is a spiritual pursuit that rewards mindfulness, not violent need, and there was nothing in Louisa's power or my own that could extract us from our predicament. Still, I grasped the seat cushions, lowered my head, and whispered prayers. The spirits were a capricious bunch, often swayed by flattery. And though I might not command their help, any assistance they chose to offer might turn the day.

We moved dangerously fast now, and when the stagecoach struck a rise in the earth, the four of us slammed our heads against the roof before crashing back into our seats.

Aubrey shrieked. "I dropped my gun!"

A hail of bullets assaulted the stage. A pair of them struck Aubrey; one pierced his forearm and the other cut a narrow groove across the side of his neck and lodged in the seat back. This only enlivened him. Aubrey went to work with his remaining pistol, shot the horse out from underneath the nearest rider. This brought down another as the first animal fell in a heap and they became entangled.

"Don't shoot any more horses!" said Hank.

"Quickest way to slow them down," said Aubrey.

"Horses ain't done nothing wrong."

"Quit talking and start shooting."

The riders were everywhere, and no amount of shooting dissuaded them for long. The stagecoach bounced and rumbled, swerved one way, then another, as either Frank or Thirsty tried to maneuver us to safety. With so many bullets blazing trails through the night, I was astonished that anyone in the driver's box still lived to keep us moving forward. Or, perhaps, that wasn't the case at all. For all I knew, Frank and Thirsty had fallen from their seats a mile back. Might be our terrified team of horses were left in charge, pulling us fast as they could, along the road to Hell.

It was as these fearful thoughts raced through my mind that the stagecoach struck something solid. Maybe a sharp rise in the earth. Maybe a lonely chunk of granite that some long-ago settler had used to mark a grave. It didn't matter. The stagecoach leapt up onto two wheels, then tumbled over. We rolled for a long time, the four of us crashing into one another with grunts and curses. There was nothing to hold on to. We came together in a collision of skulls and bones. When we finally stopped moving, the world was momentarily silent. Then the sound of gunfire caught up with us, and I could hear someone outside screaming.

The stagecoach had come to rest on one side; Aubrey pushed upward at once and threw open the coach doors. My instinct was to hide there in the relative safety of the coach's interior, but of course those hunting us could simply approach and shoot us while we huddled in fear. Aubrey intended to fight, and we had little choice but to join him. Mabel was covered in blood, and I could not tell if her wounds had begun spilling again, or if the blood belonged to someone else. Every part of me ached, and I'd managed to bite through my bottom lip. Blood leaked down Hank's forehead, and he clasped his Peacemaker against his chest as if holding tight to his only child. His eyes were wild, and I'm not certain he knew yet that we'd stopped rolling. I wanted to examine them both for injuries, examine myself too, but there was no time. Aubrey was firing into the distance, and Mabel rose in a hurry and joined him.

I worked myself into a standing position so I could survey the battle.

Night still reigned, but the first blade of sunlight sliced across the far horizon. The stagecoach was splintered and smashed; all the wheels had snapped off their axles. Of the four horses that formed our team, three lay dead and bound up in the riggings. The fourth shrieked and thrashed, slammed its head in the ground over and over, but could not escape the wreckage. I think, perhaps, its legs were snapped. Our pursuers surrounded us, racing in circles around the broken coach. Between the streaking torchlight and the constant gun smoke, I could discern no faces, only shadowy forms that ran together into a great black lasso that drew tight around us all. I might have spied Sheriff Bramlett's broken face in that black mass, or the righteous gleam in Preacher Branch's eyes. Might have recognized the deputies we'd jailed, or the quiet fellow who'd sold us our clothes for the fair, or the barback who worked the Silver Ace when Brick was passed out. It could have been any of them, or none of them.

Ultimately, who they were did not matter.

They'd come to kill us, and we were at their mercy.

Miraculously, Thirsty Picket had survived the tumble, and was on his knees, less than ten feet from the coach. He was busy with his rifle, moving the lever and returning fire as fast as he could. Frank stood beside him, waving his arms, and hollering. Doing his best, I realized, to draw fire to himself. Hoping to absorb every shot, and spare the rest of us. A bullet whistled close, clipped my ear. Hank tried to stand, and I shoved him back down into the coach, perhaps the first real flash of maternal instinct I'd ever felt in this world. We might all die, but there was no need for a boy of fourteen to lose his life before the rest of us.

I resumed my prayers, begged whatever spirits ruled this place to come to my aid. Wrapped my arms around Hank in hopes of shielding him from the horror.

A bullet found Thirsty. Struck him in the forehead and cut clean through his brain.

Frank picked up the dead man's rifle, began firing. He staggered about as the posse harried him with bullets.

Mabel took a shot through the shoulder. It followed the same course as the one Sheriff Bramlett had given her. Blood erupted from the old wound, and Mabel retreated into the coach, knelt there crying with her head down, clutching her rifle with the barrel pointed at the sky.

I kept low, tried to peer out. My prayers continued, and my eyes cast about for any sign that the universe was coming to our aid.

Aubrey stood tall, crawled on top of the upturned coach, and continued firing like a wild man. So far, he'd avoided further injury, and I wondered if indeed the spirits had intervened, or if this was simply the same foolish luck that had carried him safely through his violent life. But as I watched him spin in circles, gun barking and his smile wide as the West itself, Aubrey's luck ran out. Several shots struck him in quick succession, and he collapsed back into the coach, hands gripping his leg to keep blood from rushing out. Aubrey was a man acquainted with trouble, and he pulled off his jacket and began the expert application of pressure and binding to his wounds.

Terrified laughter surfaced, and I couldn't hold it back. I clapped my hand over my mouth. Swallowed the laughter and mumbled prayers into my palms, no longer begging for aid but *demanding* it.

I risked another look and saw Frank fall to his knees, succumbing to the withering fire.

And then, along that golden horizon, I saw them.

Spirits. Demons. Angels with fiery swords, riding forth to rid the earth of our enemies.

No.

These were riders of the human variety, racing toward us with the rising sun at their backs. A dozen. Two dozen. More. They unleashed rifle fire, and I could hear their shots hissing in the air.

So did the men trying to kill us.

Their attack lost form, and they reined around to face this looming threat. When our saviors came fully into view, I gave a whoop of joy. These were the people of *Cowboy Dan's Wild West Revue*, racing across the prairie like floodwaters unleashed from the departed storm. Old time cowboys and trick riders. Sharpshooters and gray-haired cavalrymen. Pawnee and Comanche and Kiowa horsemen, their ponies still painted from the last performance.

These were friends.

I ducked back into the coach, pulled the doors closed over our heads, and held Hank close against me as the men who'd come to kill us tried vainly to defend themselves.

The conflict did not last long. The riders of the Wild West Revue visited in greater numbers, possessed greater skill. There was a quick period of gunplay and shouting and hammering hoofbeats.

Then a silence, pure as the morning.

A knock at the stagecoach door.

"Hello in the coach," said a voice. "Anyone alive? We have routed the villains."

Cautiously, I pushed up the door, let sunshine pour into our fearful space like golden honey spilling from the comb.

People congregated around the opening, peered down at us, seeking survivors.

A man held out his hand. "It's okay, Dr. Coldbridge. You can emerge. They are all dead."

The sun blinded me, and when I tried to wipe the confusion from my eyes, I only managed to smear them with blood.

The man spoke again. "Catherine. You are okay."

And I recognized Falling Bird, his black suit now dusty and torn, his redemptive hand extended toward me.

Only then did I begin to cry.

Only then did I truly believe in miracles.

There were so many dead, we did not bother to count them. They lay strewn across the prairie, flattening the tall yellow grass and coloring it with their blood. They died torn with bullets and feathered with arrows. A few stared into the dirt, while others faced the sky, but I made no attempts to identify any of them.

Such consideration was more than they deserved.

Those of us inside the stagecoach emerged, took tentative steps back into the living world. Reluctant as baby cows on new, spindly legs. The morning was aswarm with horses. They trotted and whinnied and chewed at the grass. A few sun-red cowboys stood in a circle around Thirsty, mumbled about digging a hole. I moved them aside, dropped down next to the old man, but he was beyond any care I could provide. Frank sat on the ground beside us, thoroughly cut through with bullet wounds. One cheek had been torn away, revealing shattered teeth. He was missing an eye as well, and blood poured from his throat. Between the bullets and the fire, Frank was utterly destroyed, and yet already the magick worked to reassemble him.

Falling Bird knelt with us, put a hand on his old friend's shoulder. "You don't look well."

Frank laughed. Spat blood. "Long day."

"How did you find us?" I asked.

Falling Bird took off his hat, wiped away the sweat from his forehead with a coat sleeve. "A stagecoach being chased by a gaggle of drunkards on horseback is not difficult to track."

"I'm grateful you came."

"I was glad to help you, Catherine. But we had our own motives as well."

"What do you mean?"

"They came through after you left. A great many of them. They fired rifles into the camp to flush everyone out. Set the tents on fire. One of them was screaming about how they meant to burn out all the witches. By the time some of us assembled to repel their attack, most of them rode out to find you. They applied rough treatment to a few folks. I don't imagine it was hard to learn what direction you'd headed."

"I'm so sorry."

"I don't blame you for the evil that lives in people's hearts."

"What about Cowboy Dan?"

Falling Bird winced. "They burned that old man alive. No reason for it I could see but meanness."

I flinched like I'd been slapped. So many people who'd gathered to help us. Dead. Every one of them deserved a permanent place on my list of guilt and sorrows.

"Can somebody help me, god dammit!"

I looked up and saw Aubrey, dragging Seth's burned body away from the stagecoach. Seth had stayed bound to the roof through the whole ordeal, but Aubrey had untied him. Seth was dead weight, and Aubrey struggled mightily. He had one arm across his own belly, like he was working to keep his insides from falling out, and the other yanked at Seth's arm. Aubrey howled and grunted with the effort, and his face was white as snowfall.

"Aubrey, he's dead." I rose and walked to Aubrey, tried to help but he slapped my hand away.

"He's alive. I just need someone to help me get him on a horse."

"You'll be dead too if you don't let me tend to you."

"I'll accept no doctoring from you," he said. "Nor any magickal ministrations. Our time together is at an end, Catherine. Our lives would be richer if we'd never met you, and I believe most everyone here would tell you the same."

I wasn't going to argue. He spoke the truth.

"That may be so, but it doesn't change things. Your brother is gone."

"You are mistaken. Look at him breathe."

Seth resembled nothing more than a tree stump burned to ash, but in the stillness of the morning, I could see the slow rise and fall of his chest, and the mumbling motion of his lips as they thirsted for air.

"Aubrey, he's better off dead," I said.

"He's better off far from you! Seth saw you for what you are. Somebody help me get my brother on one of these god damn horses!"

A few of the cowboys responded to Aubrey's plea. Together they hefted Seth over the back of a tired Spanish mustang, so that his body dangled there on his belly like saddle bags, arms falling on one side of the animal, legs on the other. They worked some ropes around him, pulled the knots tight, and judged him ready to ride. Aubrey fought his way into the saddle of a second horse, blood leaking down the front of his pants. He sat low, hunched over and heaving for breath. With one last look my way, he grabbed the reins of Seth's mustang, and spurred his own horse into a trot. They departed the scene without goodbyes, and whither they headed, I cannot say.

Over the course of several hours, a grave was dug, and Thirsty Picket was laid to rest. There was talk of taking him someplace else, for a more formal burial, but it was decided this spot was as good as any. Thirsty would be happy most anywhere, so long as his grave resided in Texas. Hank repeated stories the old cowboy had told him, about his adventurous youth, when Texas was still wild and the vastness of the land was terrible and irresistible, all at once. Tall tales about close scrapes with violent creatures, human and otherwise, and though the stories were hard to credit, they were impossible to dismiss entirely.

As the afternoon grew long, everyone began to question what direction called to them. The Wild West Revue had been effectively destroyed, and the world was large.

Possibilities overwhelmed us all.

Frank sought me out as I stood staring toward the horizon, feeling for the first time in years as if nothing called me to action. No vengeance or vice or whispering voice demanded my attention.

"Where do you plan to go?" asked Frank.

"I don't know. No place really feels like home."

"You have always found your way."

"When you're forever lost, it's a skill you develop."

"Maybe you should seek out Louisa. Make amends."

"Louisa is dead."

"God, I'm sorry."

"Nothing can be done about it."

"You have friends now, I think," said Frank. "These people have grown fond of you."

"Might be they are now, but you and I have business yet. That's why you're still here, right? How do you think they'll feel when I consent to your wishes?"

"They'll understand."

"Hank won't."

"I'll talk to him."

I shook my head. "Better if he finds out when the deed is already done."

Choices were available to me. I could leave Frank there to live on, my promise unfulfilled. I could remind him that the Silver Ace had burned down around my bag, my leather book, and all my belongings. That scrap of paper where Louisa had scribbled her spell included.

It was a ready-made excuse.

But Louisa lived on with me now, and pulling those words from inside myself was easy as closing my eyes and taking a breath.

Frank deserved more than I could give him, but at the very least, he deserved his death.

"Can we just rest for a bit?" I asked.

"Of course."

We sat together in the grass. Frank leaned against a gnarled oak, and I leaned against his chest, so that I could hear the steady movement of his heart.

"There's no changing your mind?" I asked.

"I'm just so tired, Catherine."

And that was that. There was nothing else that needed saying between us. Frank and I were both worn down to our bones.

There was no ritual this time. No candles or summoning circles or arcane symbols. Letting Frank go was as easy as saying the words. And by the time the others discovered what I'd done, it was too late for arguments.

The Unkillable Frank Lightning was dead, and he would not rise again.

Epilogue: The Cold Embrace of Age

Chicago, Illinois
Winter 1923

THE MARQUEE LIGHTS of the Biograph Theater colored the Chicago snowscape shimmering shades of gold and red. Close to a foot of the stuff had fallen overnight, and flakes had continued their slow drift from the heavens through most of the morning, but the weather did not dissuade the populace from their jobs and their outdoor pursuits. Cold was a way of life in Chicago, and snow like this no more than a mild nuisance. Paths had been trod through the slush by the comings and goings of these people, and I lent my footsteps to the effort, tapping my cane ahead to make sure there was no ice lurking to trap me. The sidewalk in front of the theater had been shoveled clean, and despite the constant ache in my bones and slow unravelling of my overall health and well-being, I had no trouble finding shelter beneath the canopy, and purchasing my movie ticket from the gum-chewing youth working the booth.

Inside, the theater was warm, and I was grateful for that, despite the bang and whistle of the furnace as it labored to pump heat into the swank interior. The matinee was mostly empty. A few children, engaged in truancy, sat with their feet on the seats in front of them. They laughed and talked too loudly, but their joy didn't bother me. Toward the back of the theater, I found a comfortable seat in which to nestle, and dug my fingers into the greasy popcorn I'd secured from the lobby.

The lights flashed a few times. Dimmed entirely.

And the projector gave off the shuddering sound that announced the start of the picture. A countdown on the screen and then the title card.

The Hurricane Kid Rides the Red River Stage.

Western pictures held little interest for me, but when I'd read the name of this one on the marquee, there was no question I would buy a ticket.

Could it possibly be?

It did not take long to find out.

Within the first few frames of film, Hank Abernathy appeared on screen, long and lean and flint-eyed, a living model of the movie cowboy ideal. White hat on his head and a long bandana hanging casually from his neck. His gun belt rode low, heavy with shells, and he wasted no time drawing twin pistols in pursuit of a gang of bank robbers. Hank was no longer a kid, but the name still worked. He possessed a youthfulness that most of us lose as we age, and though he must now have been in his early thirties, I would have shaved at least ten years off that number had I spied him on the street. His long-sleeve shirt sported buttoned pockets, and I wondered if he still kept his mother's iron nail pressed close to his heart. Might be her magic kept him young. Might be just be a familial trait. But as I watched him amble across the massive screen, I could not reach a conclusion on which of those possibilities was preferable.

Eternal youth or the ability to grow old and die.

Being north of seventy now myself, I could attest to the allure of an eventual end.

My life was not without joy. But I did not care to live it forever.

Hank was an old memory to me, but one I revisited often with a mixture of bliss and melancholy. I'd not seen him since the day we buried Frank Humble. We put my late husband to rest beneath the lonely stand of ponderosa pines where we'd pledged our lives to one another, all those many years before. The old fort had been decommissioned by then, but most of the buildings remained, if only to house all the ghosts that called the land home.

We traded stories over Frank's grave. Falling Bird spoke at length of their time together in the Army, and the brotherhood that formed between them during those years. He regaled us with tales of foolhardy behavior and ugly battle, where they'd saved one another's lives, time and again. Mabel remembered Frank as a quiet gentleman, always quick with a kind word and a laugh. When she'd joined the Wild West Revue, Frank had embraced her as a little sister, and helped her acclimate to the chaos of the traveling life. Hank kept quiet. Frank had become close to a father, and whatever memories the boy cherished, he had no wish to share them.

These people, with whom I'd endured so much struggle, and of whom I'd grown so fond, left Montana the next day, and I never saw any of them again.

Mabel and Falling Bird understood what I'd done, but could no longer see me as anything but Frank's killer.

Hank regarded me with cold-eyed silence.

He had nothing to offer me but hate.

It's a strange thing to know how much someone despises you, and still somehow delight in their memory.

On the screen, the Hurricane Kid had dispatched the bank

robbers in short order, and now rode shotgun on a stagecoach called *Glitter River*. The Kid was a celebrated Texas Ranger, the only man south of the Red River capable enough to see the stage safely through Comanche territory. Within the coach rode a collection of eastern dandies and Ophelia Blake, the beautiful daughter of a wealthy steel magnate. Anyone with enough sense to find their way to a theater seat knew Ophelia and the Kid would fall in love before the end of the show, but there would be many entertaining trials for them to endure before they reached their happy ending.

When the climax arrived, the stagecoach driver, an ancient cowboy with no teeth and a joke for every occasion, managed to turn the vehicle too sharply as they were pursued, and it careened over onto its side. The driver broke his neck. Ophelia was imperiled. The dandies were of no use. But the Hurricane Kid stood tall atop the fallen coach, pistols blazing in the sunshine as the bloodthirsty Comanches rode down on him en masse. Despite their evident horsemanship, and their massive numbers, the Comanches didn't stand a chance. The Kid kept those guns blazing until every one of them was dead, then he reached down into the stagecoach and helped his beloved from the darkness, out into the light. They kissed against a backdrop of towering flat-topped peaks. This was a scenic vista that existed nowhere within the state of Texas, but one that conjured that place in the popular imagination as surely as longhorn cattle drives and tall, handsome heroes in white hats.

The West had embraced its myths.

There was no overcoming that violent momentum now.

When the Hurricane Kid pulled away from his kiss, and smiled into the eyes of his one true love, it opened a part of me that had been closed for years. Tears welled in my eyes, and spilled down my face. A powerful loneliness found me there in the shimmering darkness, and I feared there was nothing I could do to stall its relentless advance.

"Not exactly a factual account of events, is it?"

The voice startled me. I'd been so invested in the romance on screen that I hadn't noticed the massive man sitting just two seats away. He wore a long, heavy coat that concealed most of his bulk, but sat so tall that he'd surely have blocked the view of anyone behind us. He was grinning at me, and even in the darkness I could see the horrible burn scars on his face.

"Oh my."

"Hey Doc." Seth Dawson hadn't aged a day. And apart from the scars that the magick hadn't entirely banished, he appeared hale and hearty.

"You're still so young."

"And you're an old lady now."

"Tactful as ever."

"Don't mean to offend, Doc. You're still a beauty."

"I was never a beauty, Seth. Why are you here? How did you find me?"

He shrugged, stretched his arms out and draped them over the seatbacks. "Me and you, we have a connection. Surprised you can't feel it. Whatever you did to bring me back, you left your mark on me. I can feel you in the world, easy as breathing. Probably would have come to you years ago, but I wasn't sure you'd want to see me. Had to work up the nerve. You didn't know I was coming? No kind of mystical *sensation* or nothing?"

"No, Seth. I abandoned my magick long ago."

"Why would you do that?"

"It was . . . overpowering. What did it ever bring me but trouble?"

"Well, it brought me a second chance. Aubrey explained to me all that happened after I died."

"Your brother lived?"

"For a short while. Maybe a day or two. Long enough to tend to me until I was awake. He was tore up bad though, from all that mess." Seth nodded up at the screen, his disgust evident. The calvary had just arrived, to ferry Ophelia and the Kid back to the fort for their wedding.

"Wish I could have done something to help him."

Seth waved me off, obviously pained by the subject.

"I tell you one thing this movie got right," he said. "That boy could outdraw anyone I ever seen."

"You were pretty fast too."

"Oh, not near fast enough."

"Seth, can you tell me what you came to say? As you pointed out so indelicately, I'm an old woman. I'm tired and this movie is about finished and I'm ready for a rest."

"Well, I just wanted to say thanks."

"For what?"

"Bringing me back to life. What else?"

"You're thankful I cursed you?"

Seth sat up quick, and he could not hide the anger my words had elicited. "My life ain't a curse. What you done to me is a pure blessing. I'm a different sort of man now, Doc. You gave me a second chance. I am a businessman. Own a small hat store in Cleveland. I am married with two boys. Oldest one I called Aubrey, though he's a sight better behaved then his namesake ever was. People think I'm a good man, mostly. None of that ever happens if you don't help me. I'm just another dead drunk who tried to kill a little kid because my pride ran too hot. Don't ever think I'm walking the earth, wishing I was dead. I want to live as long as I can, and you're the one made that possible."

Never had I considered such a response. Seth was so animated by his gratitude, that I hadn't the heart to ask what he would do when his young wife grew old and withered away to bones, while he still worked the counter of his hat shop looking not a day older than forty. What would happen when Seth's children grew older than he was, and he was left in the unenviable position of counting down the days until they were dead too?

Seth was so thrilled with his life, so pure in his desire to live it.

Perhaps that would be enough. For a time.

What did I truly know? I'd obsessed over death for so long, I never learned to obsess over life.

"Thank you, Doc," he said.

"You are so very welcome."

Our business concluded, Seth placed a top hat on his head and rose. "If I can ever do anything."

"I'll keep that in mind."

After Seth departed, I bought a ticket for the next showing. Watched the whole movie again, and wished for all the lives I'd never gotten to live.

When I left the theater, the snow had resumed falling in earnest, and the pathways cut by the stomping of feet and the slow passage of cars were rapidly refilling.

Bathed in the lights of the marquee, I turned my eyes to the gray skies. Breathed in the blistering cold.

Easy as turning on a light switch, the words came to me, and I whispered a prayer of forgiveness.

And the magick welcomed me home.

The magick had never left me.

My loves were still there. Not within my reach, not yet, but so very close. I could hear their laughter echoing through the streets and feel their touch in every breath of wind.

And I knew, one day, they'd embrace me again.

There, in that beautiful forever, from which none of us ever return.

Afterword

I DON'T KNOW where this all started. Maybe with all the Western paperbacks I read when I was a kid. Maybe with all the monster movies I used to watch on Saturday afternoon television. Growing up in rural West Texas, the Old West is still so close, you can taste the trail dust in your teeth.

So, a few years back, I set out to write some monster stories set in old Texas, a period I defined as roughly 1830 to 1930. These would be classic monster stories, set in mostly nontraditional western settings. By that I mean, in the West as it *really* was, not the mythological West that most of us envision.

And that's the thing, the Old West as it has been popularized never really existed. Sure, there were outlaws and sheriffs and native tribes fighting for their lives against Manifest Destiny. There were cattle drives and wagon trains and train robberies.

But most of that was filtered through Hollywood romance.

Life in the West had its joys, but for most, it was a hardscrabble existence. Painful and frightening. Often grim. And for the natives who endured the invasion of their homes and the death of their way of life, it was even worse.

All our familiar Old West archetypes are fun to play with, but it's more important, I think, to bring fully realized people to the page.

So, I wrote a half dozen or so stories, with all this in mind. And I loved them. I started with a story about a German immigrant in central Texas, fighting to keep what's left of her family safe from a werewolf, and from entirely human monsters. I followed that up with one about a witch, desperately trying to escape her abusive husband and bring her child back from the dead. Pretty soon I had stories about false gods, murder cults, and mermaid rebellions.

Then I took a stab at one of my favorite monsters, the Creature from the Black Lagoon. I quickly figured out he'd be right at home during the 1900 hurricane that destroyed the city of Galveston. What started as just another short story turned into a novel, *The Legend of Charlie Fish*, and I soon realized I'd tapped into the heart of the universe I was trying to create.

See, all these stories exist in my own mythological Texas, but now I started seeing places where characters from one book might bleed into another. And I had a whole lot of readers asking what happened to my young gunslinger, Hank Abernathy. Was he really dead? Did he go off into the ocean to live with Charlie?

I wasn't sure myself, so I had to find out.

Enter *The Unkillable Frank Lightning*.

Or, as my elevator pitch goes: Frankenstein in a Wild West show.

Wild West shows were travelling performances that began in the 1870's and continued well into the early twentieth century. They featured trick riders and sharpshooters, reenactments of famous battles, parades of cattle and buffalo, grand orations, and spirited horse races. For those who'd never set foot in the West, these shows brought the spectacle to them. Not as it really was, but the way people *imagined* it was.

People started selling the idea of the Old West well before that period was even finished. Ned Buntline and other dime novelists told sensational stories about the West that resembled nothing more than tall tales. People back east devoured these stories, and they drew their images of the land west of the Mississippi from dynamic artists like Frederic Remington and Charles M. Russell.

When Buffalo Bill and others came along with their Wild West shows, they leaned into the legends, and distilled all these notions of the West into pure spectacle. This stylized version of the Old West would continue into movies, and inform what many of us still believe about the West today.

In *The Unkillable Frank Lightning*, I wanted to lift the curtain a bit, and examine the inner workings of these shows. The character of Frank seemed ready-made for life as a performer, but it was Hank that drew me in all the way, and his path from wandering orphan to sideshow gunslinger to Hollywood movie star became the through line for everything I wanted to say about the mythical nature of the Old West. Catherine sees through the spectacle to the truth of the matter, and condemns it as a celebration of violence, but of course she already understands that violence lives at the very core of the American ideal, whether we want to admit it or not.

Wild West shows just made it a little bit easier to swallow.

It's the reality of the violence and the surety of death that separates the true West from the idealized version. When the lawman shoots the outlaw in the dusty middle of Main Street, the dead man is stuffed in a pine coffin, and everyone celebrates. But real violence leaves a mark. It causes trauma that's not easily overcome. The killing weighs on the killer and blood stains the ground for a long time to come.

While I love all the old Hollywood Westerns, my favorites are those that deal with the hard reality of the West without flinching. They show the fallout. They understand these characters have been broken forever.

And yeah, in *The Unkillable Frank Lightning*, even those with a relatively happy ending are scarred for life.

Broken forever.

But I think they'll persevere. I haven't finished with my Texas monster stories yet. Not sure I ever will. But I'm hoping we'll see more of Hank and Catherine at some point, and a few of the friends they've made along the way.

There are all sorts of lurking creatures that haven't yet made an appearance. Each of them every bit as terrifying and every bit as *fictional* as the Old West itself.

Hopefully if the stories are good enough, you'll believe in *both*.

Acknowledgments

Thanks to my wife Kristin, my kids, and the rest of my family for always supporting my writing, even on the days when I spend hours staring off into space. Sometimes the muse is hard to find, but you're always willing to help me look for it.

Thanks to Rick Klaw once again for helping me put the bones of the book together in the right order, and to the whole team at Tachyon: Jacob Weisman, Jill Roberts, Kasey Lansdale, Jaymee Goh, and Elizabeth Story. It's been an absolute blast working with you all, and I'm grateful for what you do.

Thanks to my agent, Kris O'Higgins, for steering the ship around every possible storm, and to my many friends in the writing world for the constant support. Special shoutout to C. S. Humble for the encouragement with this book, and to Brandy Whitten for the magical assistance.

Finally, thanks to the readers, librarians, podcasters, reviewers, and bookstores who champion the cause of books they love. Y'all are the absolute best.

JOSH ROUNTREE is a novelist and short-story writer who writes across multiple genres, focusing mostly on horror and dark fantasy. His novel *The Legend of Charlie Fish* was released by Tachyon Publications in 2023 to wide acclaim, making the *Locus* Recommended Reading List, and being named one of Los Angeles Public Library blog's best books of the year.

More than seventy of his short stories have been published in a variety of venues, including *The Deadlands*, *Beneath Ceaseless Skies*, *Bourbon Penn*, *Realms of Fantasy*, *PseudoPod*, *Weird Horror*, and *The Year's Best Dark Fantasy & Horror*. Several collections of his short fiction have been published, including *Fantastic Americana*, and most recently, *Death Aesthetic*, featuring tales of death and transformation.

Rountree lives in the greater Austin, Texas metro with his lovely wife of many years, and a pair of half-feral dogs who command his obedience.